strictly temporary

volumes one and two

Happy Reading xo Elle

ELLA FOX

Strictly Temporary, Volumes One and Two
Copyright © Ella Fox 2015

All rights reserved.

No part of this book may be reproduced or transmitted in any form or by any means, electronic or mechanical, including photocopying, recording, or by any information storage and retrieval system without the written permission of the author. This book is a work of fiction. Names, characters, places, and incidents either are the products of the author's imagination or are used fictitiously. Any resemblance to actual persons, living or dead, events, or locations is entirely coincidental.

All rights reserved. Except as permitted under the U.S. Copyright Act of 1976, no part of this publication may be reproduced, distributed, or transmitted in any form or by any means, or stored in a database or retrieval system, without the prior express, written consent of the author.

This book is intended for mature adults only.

ISBN-13:978-1508824466
ISBN-10:1508824460

Cover Design by Sommer Stein with Perfect Pear Creative Covers
Cover Photography by Sara Eirew
Cover Models Jennie Lyne and Philippe Lemire
Editing by Gemma Rowlands
Formatting by Champagne Formats

Champagne Formats

strictly temporary

volume one

USA Today Bestselling Author

ELLA FOX

dedication

To anyone that's had to deal with small town idiocy. Always remember that small-minded haters tend to congregate together.

Then, at the first available opportunity, get away from that kind of toxic crap.

Change is good. Taking big chances results in big rewards.

I'm living proof.

The Past
Just a Small Towne Girl

chapter one

IT WAS A TYPICAL and uneventful Friday night that found me behind the register at Book Me, Babe. My job at the local bookstore might not have seemed like much to anyone else, but to me it was a great fit. Aside from the obvious—being surrounded by books and people that loved them—the biggest perk was the employee discount. Having been a book addict practically since birth, being able to get twice the number of books for the money was a reason to get excited.

At the time, I was finishing up my second year of college but unlike the other college kids my age, I actually enjoyed working on Friday nights as opposed to doing keg stands and making questionable choices. My grandpa had always claimed that I was an old soul, and I guess the fact that I worked the way I did and avoided awkward social interactions meant that there was some truth to those words. I didn't feel old, but I also didn't feel the need to be flat on my back working my way through the football team in order to feel good about myself.

My lack of desire to let loose and go wild like that was absolutely a direct result of having been born, raised and judged in a town that was so uptight that mining for diamonds in someone's ass cheeks would very likely have born fruit. What made me such a target in the town? The fact that my mom had gotten pregnant by a boy who came to work on one of the town farms one summer. Although there were other pregnant girls in her high school, she was the only one that had made the mistake of carrying on with someone not from Small Towne. That basically earned her a scarlet letter and meant that I was born with one too.

Prejudice and shitty behavior run through Small Towne like a plague so of course I had to hear pretty much every day of my life that I was trash. Bullying is infectious—when no one speaks up or steps in, people get the idea that they should join in. I was an easy target and the kids I went to school with basically saw treating me like shit as a way for them to earn cool points.

After high school I'd moved twenty miles away from Small Towne—yes, that's really the name of the town, I'm sure you've been wondering—and I loved finally being able to relax after having spent eighteen years being talked about, looked at and judged almost every day. Interestingly enough most of the kids that I went to high school with didn't move on to college and the few that did had gone to State College. I was relieved not to have to see anyone from Small Towne and I flourished.

My mom and I didn't have what you would call a super close relationship—which isn't to say that she was abusive, because she wasn't—but the one thing she had always made sure of was that I knew that there was a life for me outside of Small Towne if I just had the courage to reach for it.

She provided for and took care of me, but she hadn't been ready to be a mother at sixteen, plain and simple. It wasn't like we didn't get along—like I said, she did her best—but I knew what the sacrifice of having me cost her so I always tried to be as low maintenance as possible. In a lot of ways, our relationship was similar to that of sisters.

The one thing that the two of us agreed on was that we both hated living in Small Towne—her more than me, for good reason. When she got pregnant with me and my sperm donor did a runner, it wasn't like she was overrun with opportunities. Even after she got her G.E.D and had the opportunity to leave, she stayed because that's where my grandparents lived and they loved having us both there. There were a few times over the years when it seemed like maybe we might move, but then life would happen and that would be that.

There was one time we actually started to pack boxes in preparation for a move. Mom was looking at an apartment for us in Bronson, but then my grandma had passed on and that left my Grandpa Eldon with only us. Moving plans were quickly squashed and we spent nine more years on the farm because he was tied to the farm that he'd been born and raised on.

The farm had been the family business for three generations, but when Grandpa passed away during winter break of my senior year of high school, Mom and I each agreed to sell it without so much as a backward glance. Even though he loved it, Grandpa had known that it wasn't for us, and he'd given his blessing many times over the years for us to let it go when the time came.

Once I was in college, my mom got busy traveling across the country with her new husband—who also happened to be her former boss, Henry. She'd been working for him in Bronson for years as his housekeeper—because of course no one in Small Towne would hire her for anything—but things changed for them when he was home recovering from knee surgery, and now they were married and on the move, and they were even talking about having a baby or two. Henry was a professional poker player, so he went where the tournaments were. I could barely keep up with them, but I was more than happy to see my mother so happy and in love.

As for me, my way out came in the form of going to college in Bronson, and I was enjoying being far enough away from Small Towne to breathe. My new life might not be setting the world ablaze, but it was the most content I'd ever felt. I was in college at Bronson University and I lived in a dorm with a girl named Heather. For the first time in my life I had a real friend who didn't drop me like a hot potato whenever the popular kids demanded that it be so. I'd been screwed over by fake friends my entire life, so having Heather was a Godsend. Being away from Small Towne had opened a whole new world to me, and I was so happy I practically skipped through each day.

I thought I'd gotten away from Small Towne for good, but back then I still had too much sweet in me and I didn't fully realize just how evil people could be.

That particular Friday night I was in my usual perch—the stool behind the counter—devouring the new Sylvia Day book when it happened.

"Hey Ardy."

Just the sound of the name alone annoyed me. Lifting my head I found myself face to face with Ricky Greenway. Ricky had been the object of my teenage affection—more like obsession—and once he and his friends figured that out, they had gone out of their way to make jokes about all of the things that Ricky was more likely *to do* than me. It was humiliating beyond belief and I'd long since learned to stop playing their games and falling for their nonsense.

Even before they found out about my crush, Ricky and his crew had always picked on me. Because of them, very few people in Small Towne called me by my full name. Instead, the name Arden had been turned into a joke. RetArden, Larden and Ardy the Retardy were the most popular of the names. The adults did nothing to stop it—so much for bullying being something that was considered bad. No matter how many times my mother or grandparents complained to the teachers and principals at my schools or went directly to the parents of the children who did it, nothing ever changed.

Instead, the adults had taken to calling me Ardy as well, and I'd grown somewhat used to it, even though I didn't like it. It drove my mother and grandpa crazy, but after a while, it was what it was and I just had to stop letting it get to me. I'd succeeded, but it hurt. The fact that Ricky was standing in front of me calling me Ardy was actually an improvement on the things that he normally called me. Still—I was in no mood to be tortured by anyone from Small Towne anymore. I was out and they couldn't do anything more to me.

At least that's what I thought.

"Ricky."

His pearly whites gleamed when he grinned at me, and I cursed genetics that the two years since I'd seen him last had only made him more handsome. The problem with Ricky was that even though he was a bully and a jerk, he was so damn cute.

"It's not the same without you in Small Towne, Ardy. How're things in the big city?"

The very last thing I wanted to do was converse with Ricky Greenway and my response spoke to that. "Bronson is hardly a big city, Ricky. What can I do for you? I have to assume that you're lost because I know darn well that you don't read."

There was a moment where I thought that I saw a flash of annoyance pass over his face, but before I could be certain, it was gone, and he was smiling again.

"I came here to see you, Ardy."

My immediate response was to call bullshit, but I wasn't a trouble starter. "Why?"

After running a hand through his perfect hair, Ricky graced me with one of his signature smiles.

"Cause I missed you, silly girl. I know I wasn't a good guy in high school Ardy, but I done changed. You leavin' Small Towne and movin' on out into the big city was the wake up call I needed. The past two years have growed me up right. Didn't know what was right in front of my nose til' you left and moved on. Now that I know, I've come to court you."

I want to tell you that I didn't get soft inside, but I'd be lying. My heartbeat sped up to triple what it had been before—but at least I wasn't dumb enough to buy what he was selling on the spot. I waffled though, because I couldn't help but think that it was the kind of thing that happened in books. Why couldn't it happen to me? Maybe Ricky had finally grown up and realized what was right in front of him the entire time.

Still, I'd been through it with him enough to know not to jump in and believe it.

"You can't really believe that I would fall for this after two years, right? If you think I'm really that dumb, you've got another thing coming. Where's your gang of followers? They can't be far because I know for certain that they're in on this charade. I left Small Towne behind, Ricky—and that includes you and your "jokes." Thanks for dropping by—the door's over there. Find someone else to mess with."

Letting out an exaggerated sigh, Ricky's shoulders drooped dejectedly. "I shoulda figured you wasn't gonna give me a chance right off."

Having been the subject of Ricky's games and manipulations before, I said nothing. He looked surprised by my lack of participation, but it didn't deter him.

"You know what I'm gonna do, Ardy? I'm gonna *prove* to you that I'm a changed man. You'll see. I'm not givin' up on what we might be, Arden Winger. I'll be back."

I had doubted it very much—but he proved me wrong. He came

back every day that I worked. A few weeks later I found out he'd called my boss and begged to know what my schedule was. Every time he came, he had one long stemmed red rose in hand from the grocery store. He emailed me several times a day and made my heart go pitter-patter from his charm.

It took him nine weeks to wear me down. By that time I was certain that it wasn't a joke because Ricky had the attention span of a toddler. He refused to give up, and that more than anything changed my mind. I finally agreed to let him take me out to the local steakhouse, but I'd kept my guard up. At least, I had it up on date one. By the end of two months of dating I was sure that I was in love with him. When Ricky kissed me, I believed that I'd fallen into a fairytale. I had visions of seeing the people in Small Towne that had been so cruel to me, and I knew that if that ever happened, they'd be nice to me because I was Ricky's girl. No more jokes, hateful taunts or downright cruelty.

Our one disagreement had been about going all the way. He got frustrated because we'd been together for over two months and I wouldn't even let him near my panties. I explained that I wasn't ever going to do anything like that before marriage and that if he didn't like it, he could lump it. He left in a huff that night but then called me the next day and apologized.

"I got respect for you Ardy-girl. You're so much better than the Small Towne trash I've been with. You keep those legs closed baby—you aren't losing me."

The following weekend Ricky dropped to one knee right in the middle of the bookstore and asked me to be his wife. We were too young for him to have a ring, but he gave me a promise that someday he'd buy me a rock that would weigh my hand down. I didn't care one bit about the lack of the ring because I was sold on the fantasy, the happily ever after.

I couldn't believe that I was going to be Mrs. Ricky Greenway. I daydreamed about our future and completely wrote off our past. It was just like all the best books, where the heroine and the hero get a second chance and fall in love. We talked about our future together and made plans. I had two weeks left in my sophomore semester and we decided to get married after my last day of classes. As soon as I finished college for the year the plan was for Ricky to move up to Bronson. We were going to get a two-bedroom apartment so that I could keep Heather as my roommate. She wasn't gung ho about Ricky to begin with, but over time she came around and was at least friendly to him.

There was one thorn in my rosebush, and that was my mom. She didn't like the Greenways and, after years of listening to me cry over how mean Ricky and his friends were to me, she was suspicious of his motives. I got mad at her for being just as judgmental and pigheaded as the folks back in Small Towne and went off. It was the first big fight Mom and I ever had, but I was a stubborn ass, mad at her for being less than supportive. As far as I was concerned, even though we didn't have a typical relationship she was still my only remaining family and I needed her support. No matter how much I argued, she didn't back down from her position that something wasn't right, and I hung up on her one night in a huff.

I had such a burr in my saddle about it that I didn't tell her that Ricky and I had decided to elope right in the Bronson County Courthouse—and that's how I wound up becoming Mrs. Ricky Greenway one Friday afternoon with Heather as my witness and no family around me. Ricky told me that his parents weren't supportive either, but he was adamant that the two of us were going to prove the world wrong.

I wore a white dress I'd gotten at the local Dress Barn and Ricky wore khakis and a white button down. I cried when he handed me a small bouquet of three red roses—just like the single stems he used to give me, and a judge married us in less than five minutes.

That night, on the bed of a room at the Motel 6, I lost my virginity to my husband. It hurt like hell but I was so set on the fairytale that I didn't care. Plus, it took less than three minutes from start to finish, so that was bearable. It didn't get any better for me the second time that we made love that night, but Ricky's grunts and groans signaled that he enjoyed it, and that was what mattered to me. I assured myself that it would get better once we had time to really get to know each other's bodies.

The following morning I woke up to the sound of voices in the room. Opening my eyes, I found myself in the middle of my worst nightmare.

The room was full of Ricky's friends—otherwise known as the people that had terrorized me during high school. All the offenders were there; Hank, Jeb, Frankie, Thomas, Ivan—and Ricky's high school girlfriend, Rhonda. Of course she was the first person to notice that I was awake.

"Aw look—little miss white trash is awake. What's up, Retardy? Thought you were too good for us didn't you, ya little bitch? It was worth lettin' my man fuck you just to have this moment right here. We done showed you!"

As she laughed she leaned into Ricky and he wrapped his arms around her. That was the moment that I realized that, once again, I'd been played by Small Towne. It had been two freaking years since we'd gotten out of high school and they hadn't changed one bit. They were all still cruel, hateful and totally devoid of any decency. What had I fallen for?

Looking me dead in the eye, Ricky laughed darkly as he spelled it out for me. "I guess I gotta give you some credit for makin' me work for that ugly snatch, but ya only proved you're as dumb as ever. Everyone was in the other room listenin' to your stupid ass cry when I busted that cherry."

Turning to his friends, Ricky held out his hand. "Rhonda and I won the bet, fuckers. We told you this bitch would never learn, but you all said she wouldn't fall for it! Pay up."

I'm not being dramatic when I tell you that at that moment I was so sick that everything seemed to happen in slow motion. One by one Hank, Jeb, Thomas and Ivan opened their wallets and handed a bill to Ricky. It wasn't until Frankie paid that I realized how much each of them had bet. He glared at me as he extracted a twenty-dollar bill, which he then slapped into Ricky's hand. As he was sliding the wallet back into his pocket, Frankie gave me a look of disgust. "Can't believe I bet that you wouldn't fall for this shit. Ya just cost me a case of beer, moron."

My body ached in places it never had before, my head was swimming, my stomach was churning and never in my entire life had I felt so stupid. It was one thing to call me names, egg my car and start rumors about me—but to *marry* me? I couldn't believe anyone had that much hatred for me to do something so vile. What had I ever done to them to deserve being treated so terribly? Tears slid down my cheeks as I looked at Ricky. I prayed that I would wake up from the nightmare

I was in. All I could think was that it couldn't really be happening.

"You married me to win a bet?"

The room erupted in laughter that went on for several seconds. After the laughter died down, Ricky nodded. "Sure did. Gonna make you pay for the divorce though, and a divorce it'll have to be seein' as how I got up in your twat twice. No matter where you go or what you do, you'll always remember me bein' your first. Figure you owe me seein' as how I had to pay for all our dates. This was an expensive bet—but it was worth every cent. You're trash, Ardy Winger. Nothin' but a stupid whore like your Momma."

Rhonda let out a harsh laugh, followed by a snort. "You're not even a pretty whore, fat ass."

To this day, I can't tell you what exactly snapped in my head at that moment—but it was huge and I swear to God I actually heard it happen. With no concern for the fact that I was naked, I sprang up from the bed and ran at Rhonda like I was the star Quarterback. I slammed into her so hard that I knew I'd be bruised, but I didn't care. It took every single person in the room to pull me off of her, and while they struggled with me I pummeled the hell out of her face. By the time they got me off, she was a bloody and sobbing mess. When I saw the damage I'd done, I smiled.

I thought fast and the second I was on my feet and had the chance I kicked Ricky as hard as I could, dead center in the crotch. He went down screaming and crying like a little bitch, and I spat in his face while he was down as I dropped my foot down on his package a few more times.

By then everyone in the room was looking at me wide-eyed in absolute terror and honestly, they were right to be scared because I can't be sure what would have happened if I'd had a weapon. The only reason I stopped kicking Ricky was because I wanted out. I barely remember getting dressed and gathering my things, but I do remember ripping my wedding dress in half before I walked to the door. No one said anything as they all stared at me wide eyed—Rhonda was bawling her eyes out and Ricky was still shaking on the floor as the rest of the gang tried to clean Rhonda up.

Turning on my heel, I glared at them all. "If you know what's good for you, each and every one of you better stay the hell away from me. If you ever so much as *breathe* within one hundred miles of me, I won't be held accountable for my actions."

I slammed the door so hard when I left that I swear I felt the shitty little motel shake. When I got to the parking lot, I realized that I had no car. I called my roommate Heather and begged for a ride. I cried most of the tears I had on Heather's shoulder that afternoon. The rest I cried out when I called my mom and told her what happened. I have to give her credit for the fact that she never once said *I told you so.*

It was when she offered to come back that I realized that I was done being near Small Towne. I needed to escape, and I decided to take action. Three days later I said goodbye to Heather, got into my car, and headed for California.

Ricky Greenway didn't just take my virginity—he destroyed my hopes and my dreams. He took my positive outlook on life and turned it into something dark. Where once I was hopeful, after that day in the Motel 6, I was as cynical as they come.

The only positive thing I can say about what happened that day in the hotel room is that I was able to get an annulment because what Ricky had done was fraud. Things are pretty shitty when being able to get an annulment is considered a positive.

The Present
Bright Lights, Big City

chapter two

I QUIETLY SURVEY THE crowd in the club with carefully concealed disdain. Places like this are nothing but glorified meat markets. Men look for the catch of the day while women lie to themselves and pretend that they're going to find their dream man.

The whole thing is laughable, really. Mr. Right? Nothing but a fairytale that some poor fool created to give the masses false hope. Word of the mythical man spread and eventually it became Urban Legend. These days it's presented as fact. *He's out there, somewhere,* or, *Someday soon my prince will come,* women whisper hopefully.

Nonsense—nothing but gobbledygook. It's no different than believing in the Tooth Fairy or Santa Claus. Bottom line—it's all made up, a fantasy that the entire female population has been force-fed since birth. So few people ever get anything that even vaguely resembles the fairytale, and I know for damn sure that I'm one of the people that will never have anything like that.

I used to devour romance novels like they were vitamins, but after that day with Ricky and his friends, I left all that behind me. I haven't touched a romance novel since then. The only books I picked up between then and now were textbooks for school. In my mind, reading was something that gave me false hope, and that made me ripe to be destroyed by Ricky and his friends. I'm a realist now, through and through.

After leaving Small Towne and landing in California, I enrolled in school. I was totally lost because I had no clue what I wanted to do, so I ended up getting a Business Degree. When I was at Bronson University I'd been enrolled as an English major. Back then I'd believed that some day I'd be writing books of my own—an idea which makes me laugh now. Right or wrong, I feel that all the reading I did warped my brain and made me a total idiot.

Meanwhile, my business degree hasn't been what you would call a barnburner, and I have to admit that I'm sort of at loose ends in that department. The bottom line is that I've got it good and I know it. Three years ago I lucked into a great job as the chief scheduling secretary for one of the biggest building firms in the world, Hart International, but I'm not sure that's what I want to do for the next forty years. The salary I make at Hart is almost double what I'd make anywhere else and I absolutely love the company, so leaving isn't really on the agenda. The irony is that if I lived in Small Towne and made what I make at Hart, I'd be one of the most successful people there. Here in LA, I'm comfortable but not enough to buy my own house because real estate here is insane.

It doesn't matter—I'd choose Los Angeles over Small Towne any day, especially working at Hart International.

Hart is a family business and I've gotten close with one of the owners. Not just close—she's become my mentor, really. Sabrina's husband is the President of the company—something you would assume means that they're rich assholes that have no time for people like me who are fairly low on the company totem pole—but they couldn't be nicer. It's clear that Sabrina knew that I needed some guidance because she took me under her wing and she's been gently trying to encourage me to go back to school. It's a conundrum because Hart pays for employees to further their education, but I have no idea what I would go for.

It's Sabrina that talked me into coming to this club. She and her ridiculously hot husband, Dante, reserved the VIP section for friends and family tonight in order to celebrate their brother Damien's birthday. It seemed like a weird choice because every one of the family members is married, but Sabrina's blush as she explained that all of the men love to dance with their women pretty much explained what was

strictly temporary

really going on.

I'm actually expending effort not to get all swoony over the fact that these people have all been married for quite a while—Sabrina and Dante are going on six years and everyone else in their family have been married for at least four—and yet here they are getting sexy with each other at a club. If they weren't so nice, I'd be pissed about how damn lucky they are.

Even with the VIP area completely blocked off for this event, it's still close quarters. The Harts aren't what you would call a small family and their extended family is enormous. Add in friends and there's a bit of a crowd for me to navigate carefully as I make my way to the bar. Clubbing might not be my thing but Sabrina insisted that I wear something sexy if for no other reason than to make myself feel good—which is why I'm making my way through the crowd in four inch spike Louboutins that she bought me for my birthday.

That crazy woman insists that a sexy pair of high heels can change your life. For me that change is likely going to result in me spending time with a chiropractor. Still, I can't lie—when I saw the Louboutin logo on the box and then got a load of the red-bottomed heels, my heart skipped a few beats. I'll never make enough money to love shoes as much as Sabrina Hart does, but I have to admit . . . these shoes kick serious ass.

The bartenders in the VIP section are incredibly attentive and within sixty seconds of placing my order I've got a chocolate martini in my hand courtesy of a girl who looks like she should be a runway model as opposed to a bartender. Color me skeptical that the drink is going to be even halfway decent. Taking a sip, I let out a low moan of pure pleasure as the perfect flavor spreads across my tongue and I mentally scold myself for judging a book by its cover. She isn't just a bartender—she's a mixologist.

I hear a groan at the same moment that I feel someone standing right at my back. It sends a shiver through me as I lower my drink.

"I've never wanted a chocolate drink before," a deep and incredibly sexy voice growls against my ear, "but listening to that moan made me want ninety of them."

I have no explanation for why my nipples immediately become so hard that they could chip diamonds, nor do I know why I've got goose bumps. I'm reasonably sure that the reason my panties are damp is because whoever he is, he smells like liquid sex. Straightening my back and mentally erecting my barriers, I turn to tell the man with the *fuck me* voice to take a hike.

As soon as I'm turned to him, I realize my error. He was too close to begin with and now, I'm right against him, looking at a pair of sexy as sin lips. Suddenly my own feel desert dry and I lick them as I continue staring at his mouth and jaw line. Sweet holy hell—this man's DNA could be bottled and sold for millions. I'm not even seeing all of his face and already I know that's he's beautiful.

A jostling from behind pushes him forward forcing us up against each other—enough so that I can feel that he's semi hard. My breath leaves me in a whoosh, as my panties get even wetter, and my inner voice is now screaming at me to run—far and fast. Taking a deep breath I raise my free hand and set it on his chest, pushing him back from me. "Don't touch me," I snap.

Lifting his hands to his side so that I can see them he says, "Don't be angry, Beautiful. I didn't mean to close in on you like that. I just wanted to meet you."

I am liquid just from listening to the husky tone of his voice, and it both annoys and terrifies me. Lifting my eyes up to check out the rest of his features, I shiver as I get a good look at the man before me. He's well over six feet tall with jet-black hair and cognac colored eyes that are sending a very sexual message. Licking my lips, I try to think of something to say, then stop dead when my brain finally engages and I realize that I'm staring at Exton freaking Alexander.

Yes, you read that correctly.

I am face to face with one of the *biggest* playboys in Hollywood, Exton Alexander. Last month the gossip that was literally everywhere claimed that he left a screening of the latest movie he wrote with ten—yes, ten—girls in tow.

Once a ridiculously adorable teen actor, Exton went from cute to sexy near overnight. After dropping out of the public eye for a few years to go to college, he came back as a screenwriter in his early twenties. He got a lot of buzz for his first movie, an Indie film that won awards at Sundance. About three months after that, the bottom dropped out when some girl he'd had sex with secretly recorded it and sold it to an Internet porn company.

Exton sued right away, but once it was out, that was that. The court case went on for a long time, but in the end he was boxed in and had to settle. Some industrious person in a promotional department capitalized on the fact that Exton's full name is Exton Xavier Alexander and dubbed him Triple X. Within six months Taken by Triple X was the most downloaded file on the Internet—quadrupling what Kim Kardashian's sex tape had done.

I haven't seen it because porn isn't really my thing, but whenever they run a story about him, TMZ always refers to him as the writer with the biggest package, so I know he's got to be working with something impressive.

It took about a year for the sex tape hubbub to die down even a little bit, and Exton refuses to comment on it in the press to this day. Once the settlement was reached, he moved on and just kept on working. Now he's known for having what they call the Midas touch with movie scripts and he hasn't written a movie that's pulled in less than one hundred million dollars in years.

You'd assume that getting caught with his pants down would've slowed his roll, but it didn't. When he's not writing blockbuster movies, Triple X is busy picking up women like he's an industrial scoop.

I normally roll my eyes when I see the gossip about him, but right now, he's pissing me off. This asshole obviously assumes that he can have anyone, anywhere, at any time.

He's wrong. He might be able to have anyone else—but he can't have me.

Without saying a word I shove him out of my way—not gently—and make my way over to where Sabrina is standing with Dante and a group of their family members. Her radar must be flawless because she looks up and spots me when I'm halfway to her. Leaning into Dante she whispers something into his ear before turning and walking to me. I ignore the small twinge of jealousy I feel when her husband runs his hand possessively down her back and palms her ass before she walks away.

The second she gets next to me, she pounces. "Arden, what's wrong? You look like you're about to light someone or something on fire."

With a flip of my hair, I shake it off. "Nothing," I say with a too-bright smile. "Everything is fine."

Eyebrow raised, she gives me a look that clearly states that she isn't buying what I'm trying to sell. I'm tempted to tell her about Exton but it's now dawning on me that he's in this VIP area with us because he must know someone here. Since Dante and Sabrina are the ones that assembled this group, chances are good that he knows one of them and I don't want to say anything that's going to bite me in the ass.

"Really," I say with a little laugh. "I guess I was just deep in thought."

"Well, then there's only one thing to do," she says with a smile.

"What's that?"

Grabbing my hand, she starts pulling me out of the VIP area with a laugh, giving me just enough time to set my chocolate martini down. Still laughing she says, "Dance!"

It takes less than two minutes for Dante to join us and within five minutes the entire Hart clan—including the extended family—is on the dance floor. They're fun and safe so being with them helps me relax. Ten minutes later I'm dancing my ass off in an attempt to forget all about Exton Alexander.

The bass thumps and the lights flash as we all dance to the beat and pretty soon my smile is as big as it gets. *This.* This is where I was meant to be. Far away from Small Towne, living a normal life in a town where people don't judge me. I might not know exactly what I want to do about going back to school, but I do know that moving to Los Angeles is the best decision I've ever made.

An adrenalin buzz has kicked in and my smile is wide as I dance. Suddenly, I feel heat at my back. Not normal warmth—this sizzles and sends a ripple of awareness up my spine. Without a doubt I know that if I turn around, Exton is going to be behind me. His sexual charge sends a jolt of desire, hot and heady, through my system, and I am struggling to shake it off.

It's been five years since Ricky ruined the course of my life, and in that time I've had sex one more time—with a nice guy named Jonas that was in my economics class. I'd slept with him about six months after arriving in LA and that was just so that I could say that I'd had sex with someone *other* than Ricky. The experience was really no better than being with Ricky and I'd quickly written sex off. All that toe-curling, back arching screaming orgasm shit? Lies. All lies. For me it was more eye-rolling, uncomfortable and borderline gross.

I'm beyond relieved that I haven't turned around and told Exton to fuck off when I see Sabrina smile and wave at him like he's one of her favorite people, immediately followed by Dante acknowledging him with a big smile. Damn, I was right—he's here at their invitation. I need to get rid of him, but I have to do it nicely.

Spinning around on my heel, I come face to face with him again, ready to meet the situation head on and tell him, in no uncertain terms, that I am not interested. The words forming in my head quickly disappear the second I see the predatory look in his eyes as he looks me over. I shouldn't be having any kind of a reaction, I know this, but I can't help myself.

It's damned near impossible not to gasp when he grips my waist firmly—but not painfully—between his hands and maneuvers me forward before leaning in close. "Dance with me," he says huskily.

When he raises his head, I see it—a look in his eyes that makes me think that he expects me to say yes. He's obviously the type that's sure of his effect on women and that makes me a little sick.

Shaking my head firmly, I smile tightly as I slowly mouth, "No thank you."

Surprise quickly flits across his face, followed by what looks like frustration. Not angry, just not happy that I'm giving him the brush off. That makes me think that I am right to assume that he isn't used to being turned down. Mentally patting myself on the back, I struggle to keep a shit-eating grin from spreading across my face. I can't lie—I'm taking some pleasure about the fact that I've surprised him.

The nod of understanding he gives me is forced, but I have to give him credit for being a gentleman and walking away. For the rest of the night I feel his eyes on me at certain points, but luckily he never says anything else.

Only later when I'm at home in the darkness of my bedroom do I admit to myself that I really did want to dance with him. I wanted to—but I am proud of myself for fighting against that desire. A man like Exton Alexander is the very last thing I need.

chapter three

"ALRIGHT, I WAITED YOU out but you're being stubborn and keeping the deets to yourself. You've got to tell me. What happened between you and Exton on Friday night?"

So much for getting one over on her. I should've known that Sabrina didn't take my response to the text she sent Saturday morning asking this very same question at face value.

"Not a thing," I say with what I hope is an air of indifference. "He asked me to dance, I said no thank you. That was it."

"I call bullshit," she answers immediately.

We're eating lunch alone together in Dante's office, something we do each week. Sabrina works Monday through Thursday and Dante works Tuesday through Friday. Unless there's a ridiculously crazy deadline or something is going on, they each work the four-day week to spend individual time with their kids. It's sickeningly adorable, to be honest, and it's only made worse by the fact that the rest of the family that works here at Hart does the same thing.

Since my own father bailed the second he heard the word pregnant, it's hard for me to wrap my mind around the fact that the Hart men take being fathers so seriously. In my heart of hearts, that's what I always wanted—the fantasy man who loves his wife, makes her feel sexy, desired and loved, and also devotes himself to being a dad. Since all of the Harts are taken, I think it's safe to say that's a wrap on the good guys in Los Angeles. Honestly, I think I just have shit luck. Even *if* Mr. Incredible were around, he wouldn't be interested in me.

"There's no bullshit about it," I say with a forced laugh. "I had no desire to be one of the many, many notches on Exton Alexander's bedpost and I'm sure that's what he was looking for. I said no thanks and that was that. I didn't even see him again for the rest of the night."

"*Sure you didn't,*" she says as she rolls her eyes dramatically. "If you never saw him watching you for the rest of the entire night, you'd have been blind or dead drunk. You were neither and I know that you definitely knew he was watching—you just pretended not to. I've never seen you so affected by a man before. Normally you just brush any signs of interest off without so much as blinking an eye. Not this time."

Waving a hand in the air dismissively, I shake it off. "It hardly matters, Rina. It's not like we'll be running into each other again."

"Well . . . about that. He called Dante last night and asked for your phone number. And just so you know—his description of you was *hot.*"

My heart is pounding so hard right now that I am surprised that Rina isn't saying anything about how loud it is. I'm dying to know what his description was, but right now I'm too freaked out that he called Dante and asked about me. What the hell am I going to do if Dante gave him my number? "Oh my God," I croak out in a panic. "*Please* tell me that Dante didn't give him my phone number!"

"Of course he didn't sweetie," she assures me calmly. "Dante would never do anything that would make you uncomfortable. You obviously didn't realize this but Exton is one of Dante's best friends—they went to college together."

Don't judge—my first reaction to the news that Dante didn't give him my number isn't one of relief. Instead, I feel . . . almost let down. At least I do until I think about the fact that they went to college together and immediately perk up as I wonder if maybe I'll see Exton again anyway.

What the hell is wrong with me?

Oblivious to my inner dialogue, Sabrina goes on. "But," she says sweetly, "He did tell him your first name and that you work here. So I'm fairly certain that he's going to search you out."

So, so many butterflies are in my stomach right now. How would

Exton look for me? Will he call and ask to speak to all of the Ardens in the building until he finds me? It wouldn't take long—there's just me.

Actually, let me take a reality check on that. I bet he'd do something real douchey like have an assistant troll the building, and I bet they'd pick up other prospects along the way. Exton Alexander looks for no one himself, I'm certain of that. And that's if he bothered to look at all. I'm surprised he asked Dante for my number. I'd say it's a safe bet it was just because he isn't used to being turned down.

"He might be a great friend for Dante, but overall he's not good news," I say firmly. "He's a man slut to the extreme and I'm not going to fall all over myself to be treated like shit. You read TMZ, Rina! You know he's got a different Victoria's Secret model under his arm every few months. They don't call him Triple X for nothing, you know . . . He's a pig."

For whatever reason, my assessment cracks her up. "Generally speaking, all men are pigs at some point. As for the Triple X thing, take that with a grain of salt. You know how LA is—there are more rumors than truths, not that I'm saying that he hasn't had a bad track record up to this point. I hope you're not judging him on that tape bullshit because no one deserves to have their privacy violated like that and I hate that people think they know what he's about because of that. I think that Exton just hasn't found his match yet, but when he does, he'll be great. You should see him with my kids. He's fabulous—he's going to be a great dad some day. Our kids love their Uncle E and Vivi especially absolutely worships him."

Holy hell—*Exton Alexander* is Uncle E? Sabrina's kids talk about Uncle E a lot. Like, a whole lot. This whole time I've just assumed Uncle E was one of the bazillion and five extended family members they've got all over the place.

"Of course I'm not judging him because of the tape—trust me, I'd be the last one to judge having some asshole betray your trust—but it's more than that with him. Being nice to children doesn't make him date material. You've had it so easy with Dante that you believe in fairytales, but that's not real life. This guy is a player, Rina. A player! *Players. Don't. Change.*"

Letting out a snort of disbelief she says, "Um—how do you imagine that Dante and I got together?"

This is an easy one. "You came in for an interview. The second you sat down in the chair, he was in love. Five minutes later he was sending truckloads of flowers to your house and he probably wrote love letters by the dozen. Anyone who sees the two of you together knows that there was never any question. I say this with love, but you're that annoyingly perfect couple that fell in love at first sight. Easiest love story ever."

Now she's straight out laughing like a crazy person. "Oh my God, Arden! You could *not* be more wrong! I hate to burst your bubble but Dante was an enormous man-whore when I met him. For the first few months that I worked here he went through women so fast that I hardly had time to remember their names. He had a three-week rule and he stuck to that like it was the eleventh commandment. It was so ridiculous that Damien and Spencer called his women the Dante-bots, not that they had any room to talk. A bigger bunch of love em' and leave em' offenders you've never seen. When Dante and I first got together, it was meant to be a temporary thing for him—the scratching of an itch. Eventually that blew up and it got so bad that I left because I didn't think it was going to work out."

I'm stunned. I can't imagine Dante Hart with anyone but Sabrina, ever. "How is that even possible? And are you seriously telling me that Damien and Spencer were like that too?"

"Yeah, I actually think they were worse. They didn't even do the three-week thing because that was *too much* of a commitment. Anyway, it's possible because that's life. People don't realize that they need something deeper until they meet the one person that changes their perspective on everything."

The Harts all make it look so easy though . . . I hardly know what to say. "You, Brooke and Delilah need to share your secret because the men you have today are the farthest thing from commitment-phobic that I've ever seen. I'd hate you all for being so damn lucky if I didn't like you so much. You've each got a gorgeous man who worships at your feet. What kind of voodoo is that?"

After taking a sip of her soda, Sabrina lets out a soft sigh. "It's love voodoo I guess. All of them just needed love—a partner to be there and support them through good times and bad. They were good men to begin with—but they didn't know that. I believe that Exton is the same way. He has this ridiculous reputation that makes him seem one way, but when you see him with his walls down, he's not like what's reported. It doesn't have to be him—I'm just saying that I think you need to get yourself out there. What're you so afraid of?"

Now that question, I can answer easily. "Falling for more bullshit," I say truthfully. "You know I don't like to discuss my past—mostly because I wish it had never happened—but once upon a time I was a giant moron and I have regretted it every single day since then. I can't ever go back to being that weak, stupid girl."

Reaching out, Sabrina settles her hand on my shoulder. "You're not weak and you're not stupid. You can't avoid living your life because of something that happened in the past, either. I'm not saying that Exton has to be the guy you take a chance on. I know the age difference could be an issue for you, so there's that. But what I *am* saying is that you can't lock yourself away forever. If it's been more than three years since the last time date night wasn't battery operated—and I know it has been because you never date—then it's time to get back out there."

This woman is a nut! Sticking my tongue out, I blow a raspberry at her. "You are so forward," I giggle.

"Eh," she says with a laugh, "There's nothing wrong with battery operated lovin.' Before Dante, I was in a committed relationship with B.O.B for a long time. Bob and his friends still like to make an appearance at the party, but it's in addition to the—"

Covering my ears with my hands, I shake my head. "Ew! No, no, no! Too much information," I sputter.

"You've seen my husband," she says in a mock-whisper. "Can you blame me for being insatiable?"

"Um, no. But I *can* blame you for making me jealous of the fact that you're married but still somehow having tons of fun in the bedroom. You know that you're the exception and not the rule, right?"

Waving the celery stick that she's holding she lets out a *hmph*. "That's all baloney, you know. My parents were still passionately in love until the day they died. The only real difference in my sex life today being married to Dante as opposed to dating him is that I have to be quieter because we have kids. If anything, I'd say our sex life is actually better now than it was back then. Which is really saying something because—"

Putting my hands together in a time out motion, I shake my head. "Noooo—none of that! Seriously, I can't take it. You're killing me here."

"Oh, you! I wasn't going to tell you anything salacious. All I was trying to say is that knowing someone and having trust makes intimacy that much better."

Yeah, sure it does—for people like Sabrina and Dante.

The second lunch was over I came back to my desk and did the dumbest thing ever.

That's right—I went onto Google and typed in *how old is Exton Alexander*. Don't judge! Sabrina mentioned the age difference and I had to find out exactly what it was, now didn't I? You know you would've done the same.

The answer is ten years. I'm twenty-five, he's thirty-five. That's a big difference, I guess—but more than the difference is the thought that it's also a little sad that he's in his mid-thirties and is still banging multiple chicks each night.

Still—and I wouldn't admit this to anyone else—there's something about the little touches of gray that are beginning to show up in his hair that is a serious turn on. There is *no* boy in Exton Alexander—he's *all man* from top to bottom and I like that far more than I should.

chapter four

THE FACT THAT IT'S almost the end of the day on Wednesday confirms what I suspected to begin with—Exton Alexander has forgotten all about me. I don't know why I got myself all worked up imagining that maybe—just maybe—he might get in contact. It's not like I wanted him to or anything. Not at all.

A soft sigh escapes me as I absently twirl a pen and think about how absolutely pathetic it is that I'm twenty-five years old and essentially fit the description of being an old maid to a T.

"Deep thoughts, Beautiful?"

Letting out a little gasp I sit straight up in a nanosecond, dropping my pen along the way. Eyes wide with shock, I find myself staring up at Exton Alexander. Holy hell, he's here, at my desk! My mind is like a hamster running on a wheel as I try to remember what the heck I'm even wearing. Welcome relief spreads through me when I recall that I'm wearing a simple azure colored blouse and a black skirt. I didn't think he'd turn up . . . but since Sabrina told me that he asked about me, for the last two days I've put a little—okay, a lot of—extra thought into my appearance. It doesn't mean anything though.

Realizing that I need to say something I blurt, "Are you here to see Mr. Hart?"

The smile that spreads across his face as he stares at me is nothing short of panty melting. I mean seriously—I think the suckers just burst into flames and disintegrated and I swear to you that the air between us is crackling with energy. What in the world is happening here?

"I'm here to see someone *far* more interesting to me than Dante," he answers.

My mouth opens, then shuts, and then opens again. No words are forthcoming, so I snap it shut without a peep. Instead of filling in the silence, he says nothing, continuing to look at me calmly as I freak the heck out inside.

Exton Alexander is at my desk . . . and he isn't here to see Dante. Also, he just called me beautiful—again. Would it be awkward if I started squealing and wringing my hands like a Southern debutante on her way to the ball while I try to make sense of what's happening?

Finally—and trust me, it's borderline awkward how long it takes for me to be able to form a coherent thought—I croak, "So you're here for . . ."

"You."

That's it. Simple, straightforward, he's just answered with one word. My mind is officially blown.

Oh. My. Lord. He's actually here for me. Am I in some kind of alternate universe?

"I don't understand . . . um . . . why?"

I swear to you, I normally have better verbal skills than this, but my ability to converse seems to have left the building. Maybe I'm dreaming. Grabbing onto that thought, I shake my head. Yes! That must be it. This whole thing—from Friday night on—must be a dream. Sliding my hand down to my knee, I lift my skirt a fraction and pinch myself. Hard.

It hurts like hell and I realize that as unbelievable as this seems, I'm actually awake. *This is really happening.*

"I couldn't stay—" he falters for a second, hands sliding into his pockets as he shakes his head. "I want to get to know you better."

"Why?"

Great—I'm so thrown off by him being here that I am now regressing to being a toddler.

Bringing one of his hands out of his pants pocket, he gestures to me. "Because I haven't been able to stop thinking of you since Friday night. Don't tell me that you don't feel the chemistry too—it all but floats in the air between us. It's the same as Friday night—so intense that I can almost see it."

Crossing my arms—because I'm cold, not because my nipples are probably—no, definitely—poking through my bra, I let out a nervous laugh all while mentally berating myself for acting like an idiot. A hot guy comes onto me and suddenly I'm all flustered.

This just won't do—time for me to get my act together and put an end to this insanity.

"You've had *chemistry* with pretty much every Victoria's Secret model for the last decade. I damn well know that I'm no model, so I'm guessing flirting with a fatty is a new way for you to get your kicks. Look, I'm not interested in your games, so I suggest that you find someone else to mind fuck. In fact, you should head off and do that now. Do you need me to validate your parking ticket?"

His head rears back and his mouth falls open for a split-second before he snaps it shut and frowns at me. "Don't talk about yourself like that, ever. You're not fat, Beautiful," he says firmly, "In fact I think you're fucking perfect. You're out of your mind if you think that you are anything less than stunning. As for the rest, I get that you've got an opinion about my past, but the majority of what you believe is based on bullshit. I'm not here to mind-fuck you. I'm here because I'd like to take you out, and if you weren't so busy building a case against me, you'd say yes. I can see that you're as affected as I am."

Oh, he's as frustrating as he is sexy.

"I'm not interested in you," I answer softly.

As he steps closer to me, I realize my mistake. Like an idiot, I've just thrown down a challenge to him. What the heck was I even thinking by saying that? I have to remind myself to swallow when he comes around my desk and squats down in front of me.

"I see you've decided to lie about what's happening here," he laughs softly.

"I'm not lying," I answer heatedly. "We're just—too far apart."

"Ah," he asks huskily. "That brings up a good point I guess—how old are you, Arden?"

"Twenty-five."

Tracing a finger up my arm, he leaves a trail of goose bumps in his wake. "I'm ten years older than you. Is that what this is about? Does that bother you?"

Shaking my head I answer truthfully. "No."

"Then there must be another reason that you're fighting this as hard as you are. Why are you lying about what you want?"

His straightforward questioning makes me defensive. "Is it really so hard for you to grasp that I'm *just not attracted to you?*"

With a tsk-tsk sound, he shakes his head. "Are you an actress?"

Swallowing past the desert in my mouth I answer simply. "No."

"That's right," he says huskily, "You're not. Which means that the chemistry between us is one hundred percent real. Your mouth likes to throw up roadblocks, but your body is a different story entirely. I'll bet every last dime I have that right now you're wet for me. Your body knows what it wants, Arden. You can lie to me, and say that isn't true, but I can see it in your eyes. You want me as much as I want you. You're fighting so hard to stay away from something that's going to be so good. Forget who you think that I am or what you've heard about me, and focus on this—right here, right now. Will you take a chance on me? Let me prove that what you think you know about me is wrong."

I want to say yes. Badly. In fact, it's hovering right on the tip of my tongue, and I'm about to go for it. Suddenly, my memory throws up a reminder of the last time someone told me that they were going to prove me wrong. That time I wound up making the biggest mistake of my life. I can't afford another go-round like that, mentally or physically.

Pushing my chair back, I stand. Looking down at him, I shake my head. "My answer is no, and it's always going to be no. It's the end of the day and I've got things to do so I'm going to go. Have a nice life!"

Without giving him a chance to say anything else, I grab my purse from under my desk and scurry away. Of course by scurry, I mean I'm half running. Nothing weird about that, right?

chapter five

After I got home and took my shower last night, I stood naked in front of my mirror and looked myself over as I tried to understand how Exton Alexander could possibly be attracted to me. Throwing that bit at him about flirting with the fatty was nothing more than a defense mechanism to me after spending most of my young life being called Larden or fat ass.

I'm not fat, but I'm not a size zero model, either. I eat food—regularly—and I've got curves. My boobs alone are ridiculously bigger than those of Exton's usual arm candy. In addition to being skinny as hell, most of the girls he's seen with have boobs that are no bigger than a small C cup and they're all tan and glowing. I'm a D cup having, size eight wearing, pale-skinned normal woman. The sun hates me so I never take on any color, my hair is long, and black, and I never color it or add highlights. Exton's women are literally high maintenance beauties—in comparison, I am essentially the exact opposite.

After I finished assessing myself, I spent last night tossing and turning like a mad woman. I was equal parts furious with and proud of myself for saying no. This morning I realized that I'm a grown ass woman and I don't need to hide from men in my apartment forever. I've never been attracted to anyone in the way that I am to Exton—what was really going to be the harm in me saying yes to a date? At worst we'd have wound up having a decent date followed by sex and it would've been as awkward and un-enjoyable as the other two times I've had sex. At best it would've been a good date followed by some decent sex and I'd at least have had the memory of the one time I cut loose and did something fun.

Or not.

It doesn't matter now though—I shot him down so I know I won't be seeing or hearing from him again.

I was tense this morning because I was sure that Sabrina was going to say something about it, but she never did. It seemed like he didn't tell her what happened yesterday, at least not yet, which was a blessing because I really didn't feel like talking about it.

In the middle of tidying up my desk so that I can leave for the day—to go home and berate myself some more—the private line straight to my desk rings. Seeing that it's Sabrina, I smile as I pick up the phone. "Hey Rina, what's up?"

She lets out what sounds like a frustrated sigh as I wait for her to answer. "So I left early to go check on the restaurant Dante's been working on in West LA . . ."

There's a long pause, so I prod her to continue. "Yeah?"

"I left my purse there and everyone is gone for the day. If I give you the door code will you pretty please with a cherry on top go pick it up and bring it to work with you tomorrow to give to Dante? I hate to ask but it's got all of my stuff in it. Dante's not answering his cell and I'm here with the kids. Vivi isn't feeling well—"

I cut her off without hesitating. "It's no problem. I'm just about to leave now. What's wrong with Vivi? Is she okay?" Vivienne is Sabrina and Dante's youngest and she's the most adorable four-year old I've ever met. They adopted her when she was three and within two months, it was like she'd been with them since birth. I'm crazy about her to be honest, and I've considered adopting a child myself one day because I can see how amazing it is for everyone involved.

Before Sabrina can respond to my question, I hear Vivi's sing song voice. "Mommy, daddy says that Uncle—"

"Crap, I have to go. Thanks for doing this, Arden, I'll message you the code right now! See you Monday. Bye!"

Without another word, Sabrina hangs up. It's unusual for her to be so short, but I guess Vivi feeling sick must have her frazzled. The poor child must have a stomach bug or something because her voice sounds just fine.

Traffic into WeHo isn't bad, so I'm at the site within twenty minutes. This is one of Dante's pet projects, so it's on his daily manifest a lot, but I've never seen it in person so I take a minute to get my bearings before approaching the door. From the outside it looks to be finished, but God only knows what I'm walking into on the inside. Hopefully it isn't too bad because I'm wearing three-inch heels and I have nothing to change into.

Stepping up to the rear door, I startle when it opens before I can enter the code. Looking up, I let out a strangled sound of shock when I find myself face to face with Exton. Again.

He looks so good in his charcoal gray pants, black shirt and gray tie that my mouth goes dry as I quickly give thanks that I didn't have sneakers to change into. In my black dress and three-inch heels I don't feel out of place, which is a relief. The problem right now is that I smell a rat.

"What're you doing here?" I ask.

Smiling, he gestures for me to come in. "I'm one of the owners," he says casually as he guides me into the restaurant.

The first thing I notice is that there is the most amazing smell wafting through the air. Dammit, I forgot to eat lunch and whatever the smell is, it's making my mouth water. Wait a second—if this is a construction site, how is it that I can smell food?

Coming to a halt beside Exton, I take the room in with wide-eyed shock. For all intents and purposes, it's finished. The majority of the tables and chairs aren't in place, but in the center of the room one round table is completely set up, right down to two full place settings.

Turning to my right, I glare at Exton. "This isn't a construction site at all. Is Sabrina's purse even here?"

God help me, the look he gives me looks a lot like a plea for understanding, and it makes me want to agree to anything he's about to say before he even has a chance to get it out.

"No," he answers carefully. "Listen, you should know that I *really* had to beg to get her to agree to help, so don't be angry with her. To be honest, she wouldn't budge so I had to call in the big guns and she really isn't happy with me right now. To be blunt, I wanted to see you again. Let's have a meal and talk. What do you say?"

The rubber is meeting the road for me right now. Last night I spent a good portion of time upset with myself for not trying something different. If I keep my guard up and I give Exton nothing to hurt me with, I'll be fine.

With a deep breath for courage, I nod. "I can't believe I'm doing this but . . . fine. I'll have dinner with you."

His smile of relief makes me feel all quivery inside. "You won't regret this," he says firmly. I shiver as he sets his hand on my lower back to guide me to the table. I'm surprised to find that my natural response is to lean into him. I only just barely manage to keep myself from doing just that.

I don't know what I was expecting, but when we get to the table he pulls the chair out for me and stands at my side like a gentleman as I settle in. Only when I'm in place does he walk around the table to sit down himself.

My heart is racing and my mind is blown because I'm sitting at a candlelit dinner table in an otherwise empty restaurant with Exton. I don't know if I can take it further than this, but I'm proud of myself for having dinner with a man for the first time in five years.

"So," I say nervously, "You own this?"

Smiling at me, he nods. "I'm what's called a silent owner. Dante and I each put up some money for our friend from college, Lazarus Charles, to start his own place."

"Oh my gosh," I say excitedly. "Lazarus is opening his own restaurant? I watched his season of Chef-Tacular! I was totally rooting for him, not that silver haired witch who screamed at everyone in the kitchen."

Nodding in agreement, Exton laughs. "He really should have won, but in the end it's probably been a blessing for him that he didn't. If he had, he'd be under contract with the Flavor Network for five years and they would've owned his ass. This way he got his name out there to a national audience and that will bring people in here. Once it gets big, and I know that it will, he'll buy Dante and I out. This was just our way to support our friend so that he could strike while the iron is hot."

I like the fact that he is supportive of his friend, a lot. It makes him more human to me—less like someone that I can think of as being just some douchebag celebrity with no real connections.

"Not only is that a great friend thing to do, it's amazing for people like me who wanted Lazarus to succeed." Toning down my excitement level a bit, I let out a nervous laugh. "Sorry, I'm a total foodie. I love to watch food shows and dream about eating in some of the restaurants they showcase."

"Don't apologize, I think it's perfect. I'm a foodie too, thanks to Laz. When we roomed together in college I didn't know the difference between a corndog and a five star meal, but he and Dante changed all of that. The meals that used to come out of the kitchen at our house were nothing short of perfection."

Shaking my head in wonder I say, "I really need to talk to Sabrina about the fact that neither she nor Dante have ever said a word about knowing either one of you. The only thing you've said so far that I did know is that Dante can cook. Sabrina says that it's one of the reasons she loves him."

We're interrupted when a server comes out and pours iced water for both of us as he confirms with Exton what bottle of wine will be paired with the appetizer. As soon as the waiter departs, he turns his attention right back to me.

"That's probably my fault," he says. "He felt like he'd failed me as a friend somehow after one of his former—uh, flings I guess you would call it—turned up at my house. Naked. She'd gone through his phone and had pulled my contact card. He felt responsible because he'd introduced me to her, but that was bullshit. She was a psycho, and he couldn't have known. Unfortunately the die was cast when that happened so he's always been a lot more tight-lipped about our friendship. I knew that Sabrina was it for him when he told me that he wanted me to meet her. While they were dating I was off in Dubai working on Snowing Sand, so when I got home and met her they were already married. Since then she's become like family to me, so I think she's as protective as he is. I know they didn't mean any offense by keeping it quiet. They both speak very highly of you."

I can't help but smile. "Oh, I didn't mean it like that. I'm not offended—I was just playing around. To be honest, it's no less than I would expect from them. If I didn't see their family coming in and out of the building, I wouldn't know that they're related to the Renegade Saints. They're not the type of people that need to brag about knowing celebrities, which only makes them that much more amazing in my book. I'll tell you what's weird though," I say with a chuckle.

Raising an eyebrow at me he asks, "What?"

"I had no idea that you were Uncle E. I started going to the kids' birthday parties and other family events over the last year but you were never there. I assumed Uncle E was a relative that lived far away."

"Ah, yes. I've missed several things this year, all because I was in Montreal while the last script I did was being shot. Now I'm stationary for the foreseeable future while I work on my next project."

As I absently run my finger around the rim of my water glass I ask, "What are you working on now?"

His eyes light up as he leans forward. "I'm working on a TV show about an underground MMA club. It's dark, violent and gritty, but I really think it's the best thing I've written in years, if not my best ever. It's exciting and different and the great thing is that with TV I'll be able to give the story a lot more depth."

I feel a twinge of jealousy about his enthusiasm for writing, but mostly I'm feeding off of his excitement. "That's awesome," I say happily. "I can tell that you're really passionate about this."

"Once I know that I'm supposed to do something, I always see it through," he replies. The fact that he looks straight into my eyes as he says it tells me that had a double meaning. I really don't know why he's so interested in me, but I can't imagine that it will last very long.

Our server interrupts us when he brings out a tray filled with plates. One by one they're set on the table and my stomach growls as I survey it all. Looking up at Exton, I shake my head in shock. "There are so many options," I say with a laugh.

Exton picks up a fork and knife as he winks at me, then slices into something and holds it up for me to take a bite. "Laz is very passionate about people enjoying his food," he says huskily. "I asked him to prepare the signature Italian feast he's famous for. You made my day when you told me that you're a fellow foodie. You can't imagine what you're in for when these flavors explode across your tongue."

Opening my mouth, I accept the forkful of food that he's offering. Closing my eyes I barely contain a sound of pure bliss as the taste of what is undoubtedly the best calamari I've ever had invades my senses. It's so good that it's actually magical.

Bite after bite of the delicious fare makes its way into both of our mouths as we continue talking about our lives. Whether intentional or not, we more or less avoid talk of the distant past, something that helps to settle my nerves. I don't talk to anyone about what happened to me in the past and I'd like to keep it that way.

We have very similar interests, including taste in movies and television. He makes me laugh with stories about living with Lazarus and Dante, and I tell him all about my Friday night food ritual with my local Chinese place and my obsession with Scentsy products. We talk about our parents and discover that neither of us have fathers in our lives. He tells me a bit about his mom, Edina, and laughs as he admits that she still refers to him as her baby boy. Once Exton graduated college, Edina moved to the Blue Ridge Mountains of North Carolina. I crack up when he tells me that her hippy-ish ways have really flourished being there, so much so that she refuses to get a cell phone because they're responsible for the downfall of society.

I tell him a little bit about my mom and my stepfather, chuckling as I admit to my complete lack of knowledge about anything poker related and how when they're telling me what's happening during the tournaments, I'm completely lost by all the lingo. He tells me that he tagged along with a professional poker player for one crazy weekend in Vegas while doing research for a script, but that he had to but it on the back burner because he just couldn't connect with the game.

By the time the entrees have been taken, I'm in food heaven. Every time there's been something new to try, Exton serves the first bite to me. I've never had a man feed me before—hell, if I had to guess the last time anyone fed me anything, I'd say it was probably my mom feeding me baby food. The first few times he did it I felt nervous about it, but now I have to admit that I'm getting used to it, and I have to admit that it's sweet. There's something sensual about it, but it's also very gentlemanly of him—which I wasn't expecting.

After all the courses are served and we've sampled everything that we possibly could—including the most amazing Italian cream cake in the history of the world—we're enjoying espressos.

Staring at me across the table, he reaches his hand out and slides it over mine. "Will you come out with me again?" He asks.

I've been calm this whole time, but now there are butterflies in my stomach. Mentally yelling at myself to keep it together, I'm silent as I get my thoughts together and assure myself that I can actually do this. Finally, I nod my agreement.

"Yes."

His responding smile is in no way cocky—instead, he just looks genuinely happy, and perhaps a bit relieved, something that immediately triggers something in my head.

"You've never had to work this hard for a date before, have you?"

Embarrassed that I've just said that out loud, I yank my hand back and cover my eyes. "Sorry, sorry—I was thinking it, I didn't mean to actually say it!"

"Stop, beautiful. There's nothing to be embarrassed about. If you want to know anything about me, you just ask. To answer your question, I'm going to shoot straight and give you the complete truth. I've never actually taken anyone on a date before, ever."

Dropping my hand from my eyes, I gape at him. "That's impossible! I've seen a bazillion pictures of you out with the Victoria's Secret model du jour."

As he rubs at his neck, I definitely notice a flush on his cheeks. "Well, that sounds fucking awful, and now I get why you assumed that I'm some kind of asshole player. To be blunt, those weren't dates. They wanted to be seen with me and have a good time, and I wanted—well, I'm sure you can imagine. It was never serious on either end and no one ever got hurt. We would go places together, but it wasn't like this. I've never asked a woman out on a date and to be honest, I've never wanted to. Not until I found you."

What does he mean when he says until I found you, I wonder to myself.

"It means that when I saw you, I immediately knew."

Wide eyed I stare at him. "Did I just think that out loud?"

He smiles at me, and then winks. "You did. I like the way you just blurt things out."

"The fact that around you I seem to have some kind of Tourette's issue doesn't make me seem . . . weird?"

"No, Beautiful. It makes you perfect. You're exactly what I need.

In fact, I think you were created just for me."

Before I can respond to that, Lazarus Charles is walking toward our table. I live in LA and I see celebrities often enough, but knowing that I'm about to meet Chef Lazarus—and be able to tell him how amazing his food is—is actually really cool.

Coming to a stop next to the table, he claps a hand down on Exton's shoulder. "I see my fine cooking saved your ass, Ex."

Throwing his head back, Exton laughs. "That it did, man. That it did. Laz, this is Arden. Arden, this is my best friend, Lazarus."

Turning to me, Lazarus holds out his arm to shake my hand. "It's a pleasure to meet the woman that finally brought this moron to his knees. You're as beautiful as he described."

I know that I'm flushing, but I can't help it. Completely glossing over what he said I say, "I can't tell you how delicious dinner was. This was the best meal I've ever had."

Lazarus stays and talks to us for a few minutes. After he leaves, Exton and I prepare to make our own exit. I'm shocked when he immediately gets to his feet and helps me from my chair.

I go into some kind of shock when he takes my hand in his and links our fingers together. When we get to my car, I'm struggling not to fidget. I'm basically struck dumb when he reaches up with his free hand and runs his fingers through my hair. "Can I see you tomorrow?"

I want to say yes, I really do, but I know that I can't, not if I want to stay emotionally unattached. With a shake of my head I say, "Not tomorrow. Maybe next week?"

Blowing out a breath, Exton looks at me with confusion. "What the hell is this about?"

Looking away from him as I pull my hand out of his, I take a deep breath. "Look, I'm not stupid. I know that this is going to be strictly temporary and I'm fine with that. You're you and I'm, well—not meant to be a part of your kind of lifestyle for long. Let's not overdo it by pretending that it's anything else. We don't need to spend a ton of time together to do what it is that we both want to do."

His harsh inhalation suggests that he's not thrilled with my answer. Sliding two of his fingers under my chin, he gently tips my face up so that I'm looking at him.

"I can't tell if you really believe the shit you're saying or if you're saying the words in the hopes that you will. For starters, anything you know about my *lifestyle* is bullshit. My last big mistake was being dumb enough to go home with a girl who forgot to tell me that in addition to wanting to fuck like she was a cheap porn star, she was looking to get her fifteen minutes of fame for doing it. Other than that, everything else you see is garbage. If you've got questions or concerns, straight up ask me and I'll tell you the truth. As for the rest of that nonsense you spewed—that's a bunch of crap. Strictly temporary, Beautiful? *That's* what you think this is?"

Swallowing past my anxiety, I nod. "That's what I *know* it is, and I'm fine with that. I don't want anything more so it's easier just to say that straight away. Everything I hear about you might not be a hundred percent true, but where there's smoke there's usually—"

He cuts me off before I can finish, covering my lips with his. I gasp involuntarily, which gives him the opportunity to slide his tongue into my mouth. My arms immediately go around his shoulders as I lean into him and meet his tongue with mine. As soon as I do, he slides one of his hands down to my hip and pulls me closer to him while at the same time backing me up against the car so that we're right up against each other.

He smells and tastes amazing and I can't help the moan that escapes my throat as he deepens the kiss. I lose track of everything as he kisses me damn near stupid. I'm wetter than I've ever been before in my life and I can't stop myself from rubbing against him suggestively. Holy hell, this man can kiss.

When he takes his mouth off mine, I groan and slide my hand into the back of his hair and try to bring him back to me. I want more—I want everything. After dropping a soft kiss on my lips, he smiles down at me.

"There's smoke and fire here, baby. If you can look me in the eye and tell me that you've ever felt anything like that, you'd be lying to both of us. This isn't some bullshit temporary thing, beautiful."

I'm getting into this too fast. Shaking my head, I push him away. "Don't crowd me, Exton. Give me space and call me next week. We'll take it from there."

He opens his mouth to say something else, but I quickly cover it with my hand so that he can't speak. "It's been a great night, please don't ruin it."

The look he gives me says that he has more to say, but instead of arguing, he nods before kissing the palm of my hand.

"Alright beautiful, I'll keep my response to myself for now. Get yourself home safely and we'll talk later."

Letting out a sigh of relief, I smile. "Thank you."

Just like in the restaurant he's a perfect gentleman, helping me into my car and closing the door once I'm inside. During the entire drive home I think about him and the kiss as I run my index finger over my swollen lips. I know that I'm doing the right thing by setting up parameters and keeping my distance. This is just the way that it has to be.

chapter six

AFTER SPENDING FORTY MINUTES in bumper-to-bumper traffic to drive the nine miles between work and home, I'm cranky and ready to relax. Throwing my keys on the counter, I blow out a deep breath and let the traffic tension go. I'm home, it's Friday and I'm about to have some great food, which I'll follow up with by doing absolutely nothing, which is exactly what I want.

Grabbing my cell, I call my favorite Chinese food restaurant to order my Friday standard. It's not depressing at all that the entire staff always knows that it's me before the phone is even picked up—thanks a lot, caller ID—or that Mrs. Tan knows that my order is a small wonton soup, an eggroll and some cashew chicken with a side of fried rice without me saying a word. It's kind of shameful that I've ordered the same exact thing almost every Friday night for the last two years. Sometimes I think that I should switch it up, but honestly the food is so darn good that I can't help myself.

A relaxed sigh escapes me as I take off my work clothes and change into a pair of yoga shorts and a tank top with a super soft tee shirt over it. After throwing my hair up into a messy bun, I go into the bathroom and scrub my face. Heading into the kitchen, I pour myself a large glass of white zinfandel. There is nothing, and I do mean nothing, like coming home, taking my bra off, getting comfortable and relaxing with a glass of wine. While I wait for the food to arrive I putter around the apartment, opening bills and wiping down the counters in the kitchen.

The bell chimes announcing the arrival of my food, and I make my way to the door to take possession of tonight's feast. Opening the door with a smile, I stop dead in my tracks when I find Exton standing there dressed in a white shirt and jeans. It takes a few seconds for me to realize that he's also holding two enormous bags in his hands.

"I, uh . . . what're you doing here," I squeak.

Stepping forward he drops a kiss on my lips. My mind is spinning when he pulls back to walk past me. Looking back at me over his shoulder he says, "Delivery."

I've no choice but to follow him as he walks down the hall toward my kitchen. When he gets there he sets the bags he's holding onto the table.

"Deliva what now?"

Chuckling quietly, he pulls a chair at the table out, motioning for me to sit down. "Delivery, Beautiful. I brought dinner."

I take a deep breath as I try to calm my nerves. Exton is in my home at my kitchen table. Holy. Hell.

"How did you get here?"

"I got in my car and drove."

Throwing my hands dramatically in the air I snap, "No shit, Sherlock. I mean how did you know where I live?"

"Oh, that," he says with a laugh. "Fact is, I went through Sabrina's Christmas card address list this morning while Vivi kept her occupied in the back yard."

"You're saying that you had a *child* cover for you so that you could snoop?"

"I sure did," he says with a smile that clearly indicates that he's not ashamed. "I'll do whatever it takes for you, Arden. Vivi's the one that got Sabrina to agree to my plan yesterday too. Vivi likes you so it's not like I had to beg her to help. She's got an angelic face and she melts hearts with her smile—which means that she's pretty much the most badass sidekick of all time."

Struggling not to laugh at that I blurt, "Well, you wasted your time because I ordered dinner already."

"I know, babe. I got it right here," he says with a wink.

Gesturing to the table, I shake my head. "I definitely didn't order all of that."

My breath catches in my throat when he throws his head back and laughs. He's so sexy that even his laugh does things to my body.

"I have your usual here, and then I ordered a bunch of other stuff. We're going to eat way too much Chinese food and maybe eat more in about two hours when we're hungry again. You know how that goes."

Sputtering stupidly, I put my hands on my hips and glare at him. "Listen buddy, I told you to call me next week! What are you doing?"

Letting go of the back of the chair he's been holding out, Exton steps toward me. I let out a squeak when he slides one of his hands down to my ass while at the same time tangling his other hand in my hair. When our mouths meet, we simultaneously let out gasps when an electric shock sparks between our lips.

Pulling my head back with the hand tangled in my hair, he looks at me with a look that I can only classify as pure sexy caveman. "You feel that, Beautiful?"

Nodding helplessly, I lick my lips and stare at him in a kind of shock.

"That's what I'm doing here. This is not the kind of thing you walk away from or leave to chance for a week—that's just not going to happen. You aren't running and I can't stay away," he says firmly.

"But—"

I get no farther as he covers my mouth with his and silences my arguments. I thought I got the full treatment from Exton's mouth and tongue last night, but it wasn't even close. He isn't just kissing me now—he's claiming and consuming me all in one fell swoop. I kiss him back mindlessly as I struggle to fight through the dizziness that I feel. My hands are running up and down the front of his shirt, feeling the city of warm muscle that it covers.

As my hands span his abs, he lets out a feral growl and I moan in response. By the time he lifts his head I'm so dizzy I feel like I might fall over. Fortunately for my balance, Exton still has a firm grip on me.

We're both breathing heavily as we stare at each other wildly. Leaning in again, he drops soft kisses along my jaw line. "You're so fucking sexy that I could feast on you for hours. If it were my call, I'd say fuck the food. You don't even realize what you do to me," he growls against my ear.

I have never had a reaction to anyone that is as visceral to the one I am having to Exton Alexander. Not even close. I want to say something back, but I just don't have any words.

When he lifts his head again, all I see is a determined certainty on his face. Taking his hands off of me, he gives me a wink. "Now that we got that out of the way, how about I feed you?"

I'm pretty sure I must've lost a fair amount of brain cells during that make-out session because instead of arguing more about the fact that he's just invited himself to dinner at my house, I let it go. Walking across the kitchen I grab another plate and some cutlery before going back to the table and setting it down all while Exton remains standing as he watches me silently. Looking up at him I ask, "Water, iced-tea or soda?"

"Which one are you having?"

Well, right now I'm having an out of body experience, but I can't tell him that. "Uh, tea I think. Yeah—iced tea."

"Then iced-tea it'll be. Come sit down and I'll get it."

Instead of arguing the fact that it's my kitchen and I know where everything is and he doesn't, I let him help me into a chair at the table. Once I've told him which cabinet the glasses are in he makes quick work of pouring tea for us. Taking a seat he starts pulling containers—a lot of containers—from the two loaded down bags he brought with him.

Gesturing to the containers with a laugh I ask, "Did you order the entire menu?"

He chuckles as he shakes his head in the negative. "I spent a few hours doing research by way of the Yelp app. You were right, by the way—this place has amazing reviews. I went through about a hundred of them and went with the things that were the highest rated. Of course I made sure to get your usual too. Mrs. Tan was very helpful."

It's a struggle to keep my mouth from falling open. "You spent a few *hours* on Yelp picking out what to eat?"

Busy opening containers, he shrugs. "I wanted to make you happy. You're laughing so I guess I did okay."

Surveying the massive selection in front of me, I let out a giggle. A giggle. I don't *giggle* in front of men, ever. What is happening to my brain? Brushing off my nerves, I reach out and choose a container. We spend a few minutes filling our plates before we start eating. Just like last night, Exton will hold his fork out for me from time to time so that I'll try some of what's on his plate.

"I've got my Apple TV down in the car," he says casually. "If you don't have Netflix I can hook it up here so we can watch something. Or I can go to the Redbox and grab a movie if you want."

Fiddling with my fork, I look at him wide-eyed. "Dinner was great, but really, you must have somewhere more exciting to be than watching TV on my couch. I know spending time with someone like me isn't your normal speed."

Setting his fork down he shakes his head. "You have got to be kidding me," he mumbles. Looking me in the eye he shakes his head in apparent frustration. "Woman, you're going to be the death of me."

"I didn't mean to insult you—"

"Actually," he says firmly, "You're insulting *yourself*. I'm exactly where I want to be and there is nothing I'd rather be doing than spending time with you. I'm really not sure what I've got to do to get that through your head, but I won't quit until you understand."

I don't quite know how to respond to that. Finally, I settle on ignoring it entirely. "I have Netflix."

"That's all you've got to say?"

Leaning back in my chair, I cross my arms defensively over my chest. "I was unaware that I needed to respond in a certain way."

The way his eyes take fire has me shifting in my seat. When his gaze drops to my chest, I look down and let out a shocked yelp. "Holy shit! Why didn't you say anything about the fact that I'm dressed like this? I look like a freaking skank!"

I'm halfway out of my seat to run into my bedroom and put something more attractive on when he stops me. "Babe, you look like a goddamn dream and you aren't changing. I like this look, a lot."

A terrible suspicion takes hold in my head. "Oh crap, now I get it. You're bored with the same old same old so you're trying something new. That has to be what this is. You're normally with models and in comparison, I look like I ate one."

Smacking his hand down on the table, Exton lets out a sound that's along the lines of being a growl. "I swear to you, the very next time you refer to yourself as being fat, I'm going to put you over my knee. You're fucking sexy as hell and you put every woman I've ever seen to shame. I'm here for *you*, Arden, not to get my fucking kicks. Don't insult either one of us by trying to cheapen shit and make this less than what it is."

He's making me crazy. In the last seven days he's managed to completely disrupt my normally quite ordinary and well-ordered life. Glaring at him I snap, "Maybe you should clue me in and tell me what the hell this is then, since you seem to be the one with all the answers!"

After staring at me silently for a few seconds and running his hand through his hair, he exhales sharply. "You're so busy fighting and spinning out that I don't think you're in the headspace to hear what I know. All you need to focus on right now is relaxing into it instead of fighting it. You're just wasting time, Beautiful."

I'm not going to lie to you—I am terrified. Only the fact that my arms are crossed in front of my chest is hiding the fact that my hands are shaking. It's like the man doesn't understand how intimidating this whole thing is to me. I really don't understand how he's so certain that this is supposed to be happening.

"I'm going to put the food away and do the dishes. Go cue up whatever it is we're going to watch tonight."

"You're the guest—"

"Babe, I'm doing this shit and you're relaxing. Don't think of me as a guest. Go pick something to watch—I'll be right there."

Accepting that it's pointless to argue semantics with him, I leave the kitchen and head for my bedroom to get changed. I'm just at the door when I hear him bellow, "Don't you even think about going to get changed, woman!"

I spin around quickly, fully expecting to find him at the other end of the hallway but he's not there. Marching back into the kitchen, I find him moving closed containers from the table to the refrigerator.

"How did you know—"

Looking over at me, he smirks. "Lucky guess."

"Ugh," I say as I turn to go to the living room. "You're really overbearing sometimes!"

The sound of his laugh is the only answer I get. Turning on the TV, I get us all ready for The Walking Dead. Once I've got that under control, I flop down on the couch.

I don't have to wait too long for him to join me, and as he enters the room my mouth goes Sahara desert dry. This man fills out a pair of jeans like nothing I've ever seen before. If I were a braver woman, I'd ask him to turn around so that I could stare at his ass for a while.

Coming to a stop just in front of me, he stays still and does nothing. Looking up at him in confusion, I find him smirking down at me. "Like what you see, Beautiful?"

Blushing furiously, I shake my head. "No . . . I mean yes. Or no!" Oh my God, I am a blubbering idiot. I know I'm failing to act cool here, but it's as if I can't stop. "Wait, I mean yes—I was just wondering what kind of jeans you're wearing. I need a new pair."

He's straight up laughing his ass off as he drops down onto the couch next to me, sliding his arm onto the back of the couch behind my head. "So you're in the market for a pair of men's jeans?"

Giving him a dirty look I snap, "You couldn't just let me salvage my pride, could you?"

"Nope. I think it's fucking hot that you're checking me out and I don't want you pretending otherwise. You know damn well that I'm looking at you and liking what I see—of course I want you to feel the same."

I have no response to that other than my rapidly beating heart. Changing the subject entirely I say, "You good with The Walking Dead? Because that's what I was planning to watch."

As he sets his feet on top of my coffee table and gets comfortable, he nods. "I told you last night I love this shit so yeah, I'm down. Let's watch some walkers get fucked up."

The man gives me no breathing room whatsoever. I try to stay a comfortable distance from him, but he isn't having it. Within about ten minutes he's got me pulled tight against him and my head is resting on his shoulder. I'm not a party animal so by the end of episode four, I'm snuggled into him and yawning my face off.

Hearing the steady thump-thump-thump of his heart combined with the rhythm of his breathing must've lulled me to sleep. I come awake like a shot, quickly realizing that the TV screen is black. At some point positions shifted and Exton is sleeping below me and we're covered with a blanket. I have a vague recollection of being the one to pull it over us, but that's it.

Immediately my heart begins racing and I start freaking out. I can't believe I let down my guard enough to fall asleep with him! The last time I fell asleep with a guy I woke up in hell. What was I thinking letting this happen? This crosses the line and makes me feel ridiculously irresponsible.

Sitting up, I get to my feet and start pushing at Exton's shoulder. "Wake up! You have to go."

It takes a few seconds to get him to wake up and when he does he opens his eyes and stares at me blankly. Eyes darting around the room, he looks back at me in confusion. "What?"

"We fell asleep. You have to go."

He lets out a yawn as he sits up and stretches his arms up over his head. "What time is it?"

Looking over my shoulder to the cable box, I let out a groan. We slept like that for at least six hours! I really need to get a hold of myself because this is quickly taking a turn to the disastrous. He makes me forget the rules that I need to live by. Looking back at him I snap, "It's four in the morning *and you have to go.*"

Reaching a hand up, Exton grabs me by the waist and pulls me down onto his lap. "Babe, you have got to stop freaking out. Nothing bad is going to happen. Pretty soon we'll be sleeping together every night and we'll be doing it naked. You need to get used to this because we *are* happening."

Immediately my fight or flight response kicks into full effect. Setting my hands on his shoulders, I try to push off of his lap. Instead of letting me go, he wraps his arms around me and holds me steady.

"You need to calm down, Beautiful. I don't know why you're having a fucking fit but you need to remember one thing—I won't ever hurt you or make you do anything that you don't want to do. You're safe with me."

"That's crap," I say hotly. "You do make me do things I don't want to do! I didn't want to have dinner last night. I didn't want you here tonight! But here you are. You're like Godzilla—you flatten everything in your way in order to get to your goal. I'm nothing but a test subject to you—you just want to see if you can talk your way into my bed before you leave!"

I say this knowing that I'm going to piss him off and that he will go, but I am so panicked right now that I don't care. I need to be alone because I am freaking out.

Instead of tossing me off his lap, Exton reaches up and cups my face between his hands. "Arden, stop it. You and I both know that you wanted all of that, you're just too stubborn or afraid to admit it. This bullshit you're throwing out right now isn't going to scare me off. Take a deep breath and look me in the eye right fucking now and tell me that you don't want to be with me. Tell me that in your heart of hearts you didn't want dinner last night, you didn't want me here tonight, and that you never want to see me again. If you can do that, I'll leave and you'll never see me again."

I can do that. No problem.

"I don't want—"

Dammit. I choke. I can't say the words. Why can't I just say it?

"I don't! I don't want . . ."

"What don't you want, Beautiful?"

I open my mouth to tell him that I don't want him and that I just want to be left alone. Instead I blurt, "I just don't want to be hurt again."

And then I burst into tears.

Enveloping me in his arms, Exton holds me while I cry. The last time I shed a tear was the day after my disastrous wedding. Since then, I've kept it all inside. Suddenly it's like I can't cry enough, and five years of tears come out in a flood, all over Exton's shirt.

"Beautiful, you need to tell me right now who hurt you because I am going to fucking destroy them. Tell me who did this to you and I'll rip that rapist piece of shit apart."

It takes a few seconds for me to get a grip on what he's saying. "I wasn't raped," I blubber. "It wasn't like that. You don't need to be mad for me."

A tiny bit of the tension in his body dissipates but he's still angry, I can tell.

"Fuck yes I do, Arden. No matter what it was that happened the bottom line is that someone hurt you," he growls, "I'm not okay with that."

Other than my mom and my college roommate, no one has ever known that anything bad happened to me. The fact that Exton cares, without even knowing details, makes me cry even harder.

I'm so upset that I don't even say anything when he shifts us so that he can stand. A second later he swings me up into his arms and starts carrying me down the hall toward the bedroom. After opening the door he lays me down on the bed and walks away. This should be a relief, but instead my silent tears come faster. He left. Of course he left! I'm a flipping nutcase—what the hell did I expect?

I startle when the light in my bathroom goes on. Realizing that he's still here, I turn my head and watch as he comes back to me with a box of tissues. Climbing into bed next to me, he pulls me against him and wipes at my tears.

"I'm not going anywhere, Beautiful. Cry it out and let it all go. Tomorrow we start fresh."

Instead of fighting him—or myself—I follow his advice and let it all out.

chapter seven

MY EYES FEEL PUFFY and I've got a mild headache. Trying to remember what happened last night, I let out a groan of absolute humiliation when I realize that I cried on Exton for a ridiculous amount of time before falling asleep.

"Good morning, Beautiful."

Holy hell, he's still here. Wow. I wasn't sure he would be. Not that I care either way. Not at all.

"Ugh," I mumble with my eyes still squeezed shut. "I'm so sorry about last—"

"Don't you even think about apologizing for anything. It was a good thing that you got it out of your system and now we're moving forward."

Covering my face with my arm, I let out a groan. "Easy for you to say considering that you aren't the one that cried a river on someone you barely know. I can't believe you didn't leave—"

"Stop that shit right now," he commands. I startle as he touches my arm and gently lifts it from over my face. "Look at me, Arden."

Opening both eyes, I blink a few times before I focus on him standing right next to the bed—shirtless. Holy shit he looks even better out of his shirt than he looked in it.

"First of all, I'm not a stranger so don't even say that shit again.

Second, I think it's pretty fucking great that you felt comfortable enough in front of me to let your guard down and get that shit out. You fight it every step of the way but deep down you fucking know what this is and the fact that you let go last night backs up me saying that. Instead of obsessing about it and thinking that it was a bad thing—let it go."

I can't help that I'm gaping at him. "Um, okay."

Nodding his approval, he smiles. "Now that we got that settled, get your sexy ass up and go brush your teeth so that I can kiss you good morning and we can start the day right."

Exton Alexander turns my brain to mush, pure and simple. Getting up from the bed I head into my bathroom to take care of business and brush my teeth.

When I finally get to my toothbrush, I notice that it's already wet. Opening the bathroom door I stick my head into my bedroom where I find him making my bed and he's still shirtless. I lose my train of thought for a second, but him staring at me inquisitively brings it back. "Why's my toothbrush wet? Please tell me you didn't drop it in the toilet," I joke.

The sexy smirk he gives me makes my pulse spike. "I used it," he says matter-of-factly.

"Well alrighty then," I reply as I shut the door. After staring down at the toothbrush for a few seconds, I put some toothpaste on it and slide it into my mouth. I don't know why but for whatever reason, sharing a toothbrush with him feels really intimate. I haven't slept in a bed with a man since Ricky—and let's face it, he was no man. Ricky was an immature little punk, nothing more than a stupid boy. Exton Alexander is a man who has now slept in my bed, and used my toothbrush.

I barely know how to process all of this.

Sitting on the sand at Point Dume in Malibu with Exton, I'm enjoying the smell of the ocean and the canyon that surrounds us. There's a magical feeling here, something I never experienced while living in Small Towne. It was Exton's idea to come out here and have In n' Out burgers for dinner, and I loved it. He surprises me, there's no two ways about it. With his face obscured by a Hart International baseball cap, he hasn't even been noticed by anyone.

He's way more tactile than I would've thought. Right now he's seated behind me and I'm reclining back on him. He's got his arms wrapped around my shoulders and I'm surprisingly relaxed, all things considered.

"I need to ask you a question," he murmurs.

Oh God . . . what is he about to throw at me? Swallowing past a lump of anxiety in my throat, I nod.

"I know you're not ready right now, and I understand that. I haven't been able to stop thinking about it since last night. I won't push, but someday will you tell me what happened that hurt you so badly?"

Tensing against him, I weigh my response. I don't talk about what happened with Ricky, ever. It's just so embarrassing. Exton has been wonderful but who knows if we'll know each other long enough for me to feel secure in sharing the entire pathetic story. I have to be realistic—I still can't really believe that anything real will come of it. But, if it does, then yes—I would have to share the story with him.

Nodding my head I answer, "If this goes anywhere, then yes. I just need time."

He sighs as he hugs me tightly from behind. "This is going somewhere, Arden. You're not ready to accept that and I get it, but whenever you say something like that, I'm always going to remind you of the truth."

I'm thankful that I'm facing away from him because it means he can't see the silly hopeful smile that spreads across my face.

We were together the entire weekend, but he didn't spend the night again. Over the course of the past thirteen days we've spent as much time together as possible—even when I've tried to say that we could probably use some space. Whenever I say that, Exton shakes his head at me like he knows something that I don't.

Every day I wonder if he'll start putting at least a little bit of distance between us, but he hasn't. Instead he makes plans for us to spend more time together, and I let him. He's just always there, and I like it. I crave hearing from him and light up when I hear the text alert and see that it's from him. And the kissing—there's nothing like it. I love his filthy mouth and the shocking things that he says and does with it, and I'm ready to do more. He's been going at my speed, but I think that we both know that I'm there—ready to go.

Sabrina has been loaded with questions about how serious this is, but I've been really vague with my answers and, bless her heart, she's been letting me get away with it. She says that seeing the smile on my face is all the info she needs to know for right now.

I want so badly to believe that there is something real happening with Exton and me, but I can never forget the humiliation I felt after being stupid enough to believe Ricky's lies. I'm doing my best to keep some kind of a wall around my heart so that I don't get hurt again, but I'm aware that I'm doing a shit job. Deep down I want Exton to prove me wrong, to be the man he seems to be, but I'm scared. I'd be a fool if I weren't.

Another sign that I'm in deep is that I buckled and gave in to his repeated requests for me to go to the soft open of Laz's restaurant with him. Up until now I've refused to go anywhere really public with him for fear of running into some paparazzi. Tonight I know there will be dozens and dozens of people there that I don't know and who will probably judge me and find me wanting, and I'm freaked out. No matter what Exton says I am not even in the same zip code as his normal arm candy and that's scarier than I care to think about.

Turning this way and that, I survey myself in the mirror. Sabrina and I left work early yesterday and spent two hours shopping so that I could pick out something fabulous for tonight, and thank god she was there for me because Exton was no help. When I asked him what I should wear he told me that I'd look gorgeous in a pair of sweatpants and a ripped tee and that he didn't want me to stress out or go to any trouble to get something new because whatever I wanted to wear was fine with him. When I shared the story with Sabrina, she laughed and told me that men never really grasp how important clothing is to women. When Exton found out we were going shopping he immediately offered up his credit card. I'm proud of him for knowing when to back down because the second the words came out of his mouth and I turned on him like a wild animal, he threw his hands up and surrendered before apologizing profusely.

I'm really glad Sabrina took me by the hand and went shopping with me. If she hadn't been able to come, I wouldn't have been as daring as I was in my choice. Having her tell me I looked like a sexy bitch gave me the courage to buy a short black dress that hugs my curves without making me look like I'm about to burst out like a container of biscuit dough. The front shows a bit of cleavage but not enough to look slutty, and the back is completely open down to my waist. My cleavage is taped into this dress like you wouldn't believe, but even I have to admit that it looks hot.

Letting out a sound of excitement as the doorbell rings I slip into the silver heels that I bought to complement the dress and hurry for the door. Swinging it open I stop dead and completely lose every thought in my head as I take in how ridiculously sexy Exton looks in a three-piece suit.

"Turn around," he growls hotly.

Without a word, I do as he instructs.

"Holy hot fuck," he says huskily as he steps in and kicks the door shut behind him. Before I can say a word he's got his hands on me as he pulls me into him and starts kissing me like we haven't seen each other in months.

Sliding my fingers into his hair I melt into him and kiss him back just as desperately. I'm unable to contain my moan of pure pleasure when he starts running his hands up and down the length of my naked back.

I groan when he pulls away, staring up at him as he looks down at me with fire in his eyes. The only sound is that of our breathing, both hot and heavy.

"If we don't leave right now," he murmurs, "I'm going to have you up against this wall and I won't stop until you've come so many times that you can't bear the idea of having even one more moment of pleasure. I've never in my life wanted anyone the way I want you, Beautiful. You bring me to my fucking knees."

I let out a strangled sound at his words—a mix of pleasure and sexual frustration. I want him to take me up against this wall, and that's not something I've ever wanted before. This is really happening—I want this man. Badly.

"Tell me if I've read the signs wrong, because you know I will never push you to take it to this level before you're ready. Is it too soon, Beautiful? I want you so fucking bad that I can't think of anything else. Are you going to let me into that tight pussy or am I jumping the gun? The choice is always yours."

"I'm ready," I answer huskily. I'm more than ready. I wish he'd take me now.

Rubbing his thumb across my lips he looks into my eyes and smiles.

"Soon, baby. So fucking soon. I can't wait to bury my tongue inside of you, can't wait to taste you and hear you scream when you come. Unfortunately for both of us, we have a commitment we have to be at, so we're going to need to leave.

Oh. My. God. I think my brain is fried. He's going to do that to me? I've never had that done before and I'd be lying if I said that I haven't wondered, but I'm also scared shitless. Still in a haze of disbelief I take the hand he offers before picking up my clutch so that we can go. Only when he reminds me that I need to lock the door do I realize that I didn't do it.

I beam at him like a lovesick teenager as we walk hand in hand to his car, a beautiful black Tesla that looks like a sexy dream. When he opens the passenger door and helps me in, I damn near swoon. Who knew that there were still gentleman alive and well in today's world?

Once he's got me settled in he shuts the door and walks around the car to get in himself. I let out a little moan as he does for two reasons: one, he looks like a god of sex in his suit and two, his car smells like him. Whatever cologne he wears has to have a pheromone or something in it because it goes right to my core and makes me crazy.

It doesn't help that I'm replaying what he said to me in my apartment on a loop. The idea of his mouth on my sex is enough to make me wetter than I've ever been in my life. Shifting in my seat, I try to think of things that don't make me want to climb into his lap and ride him like an insane woman.

Reaching out, Exton picks my left hand up from my lap and entwines our fingers. "What're you thinking about, Beautiful?"

Thank goodness we're in a darkened car because I know my face is flushing. "I was just thinking about dinner," I answer.

Lifting our hands, he kisses the back of mine and then draws some kind of pattern on it with his tongue. Holding in a gasp I clench my inner muscles as I feel myself go from just wet to soaked.

"I'm thinking about eating too," he growls. "Tonight I'm going to spread those sweet legs and eat your pussy like I've been desperate to do since the night we met. I'm dying to taste you, Beautiful. Are you ready to let me fuck you with my tongue?"

Squeezing his hand, I let out a helpless sound as I nod.

"Are you wet right now, baby?"

I let out a little gasp that ends with, "Yes."

Letting go of my hand, he sets his hand on my knee and starts sliding his finger slowly—so incredibly slowly—up my thigh. "Can I taste?"

Gasping, I look over at him in shock. "Here?"

Pushing my dress up just enough to grant access, he slides his fingers over my panties.

"Fuck, you're so wet," he says huskily. "Say yes. Let me make you come."

I'd tell him he could have all of my worldly goods right now if he asked.

"Yesss," I sigh out on a moan.

A strangled cry escapes me as he pushes my panties aside and slides his fingers over my clit. "Oh shit," he groans. "I didn't think you could get sexier but feeling this little bit of hair makes me want you more. Fuck! I want to see it, need to taste it. I want to know every fucking inch of your tight, hot pussy."

Arching my back, I push myself against his fingers.

There's something about being in this small enclosed space, his fingers on my pussy as other cars fly by, that is making me so hot that I feel I might just combust. Spreading my legs as wide as I can, I cry out when he slides a finger inside of me and starts gliding it in and out while his thumb continues to work my clit. I never make myself feel as good when I do this myself, ever.

Letting out a yell of impatience, I damn near cry as he pulls his hand away. Turning to ask why he's stopped, I almost stop breathing when he sucks the finger that was just inside of me.

"Goddammit it," he growls. Bringing his finger out of his mouth, he grabs the steering wheel in a death grip with both hands.

I let out a little "Oh," sound as he floors it, then lose the ability to think when he pulls over to the side of the road with a squeal of brakes and tires.

There isn't even time to ask him what he's doing. Unbuckling his seatbelt he reaches out his left arm and then guides my face to his. His mouth meets mine in a kiss that is pure sex at the same moment that his hand pushes my panties back to the side so that he can start using his fingers on me again.

The taste of me on his lips is like an aphrodisiac and I thrust against his hand frantically as our tongues duel. Pulling out the one finger he's been working inside of me, he slides back in with two and starts working my pussy hard. His thumb is hitting just the right spot and I'm so close I can barely breathe.

Curling his fingers inside of me, he rubs against a spot that I've never found myself. Pulling my mouth away from his, I let out a strangled sound as my orgasm slams into me. "Exton, Exton, Exton," I chant as my head rocks back and forth and his fingers just keep plunging in and out of me.

"Again, baby. Again."

Shaking my head frantically I cry out. "I can't! I can never—"

"You do now. Fuck my fingers, Arden. Think about how my cock is going to stretch this pussy so fucking good. I'm going to go hard, baby. You'll scream so fucking loud and you'll beg for me to stop, then not to stop, as you come over and over again. You're so fucking wet, I know you need to come again. Feel that pussy clenching so tight—"

I come again on a wave of pleasure that is so extreme it almost hurts. This time I scream, and he groans so loud at the sound that I would have to be an idiot not to know how turned on he is right now. I shiver as he pulls his fingers out and watch in some kind of haze as he opens his glove compartment and digs around for a minute.

"Ah ha," he says triumphantly as he holds up a travel size tissue pack. I'm completely stunned as he takes care of me before pulling my panties over so that they're back in place. Dropping soft kisses around my face, he lets me come down in silence.

"Thank you for that, Beautiful. That was amazing."

Leaning into him, I laugh softly. "It was, but I feel like I should take care of—"

Cutting me off he growls, "I wouldn't be able to stop if you put your hands on me. Don't worry baby. I'll be fine by the time we get to the restaurant. Later tonight, though . . . fuck. If I think about it I'll probably break the goddamn steering wheel."

"You're hilarious," I laugh.

"I'm serious. You have no idea what you do to me."

Cupping my face, he turns me so that we're face to face. "I've never wanted anyone as much I as want you—not even close. I've never needed anyone at all, but I need you. Someday soon you'll understand that."

Dropping a soft kiss on my lips, he pulls away and turns the car back on, leaving me in a stunned silence as he merges back into traffic. Is it really possible that he feels the way that I do? I just don't know if I can let down my guard enough to really let him in. I'm infatuated and very interested in him—clearly he gets to me sexually in a way no one ever has—but does he see this going somewhere serious? Or is he playing me to get what he wants?

Grabbing my small makeup kit from my clutch, I quickly fix my lipstick and make sure that my hair is still okay. Opening the side pocket of my bag I let out a sound of victory when I pull out a plastic baggy with a few makeup removing towelettes. Opening one, I pass it to Exton.

"What's this for?"

It's slightly embarrassing but totally necessary. "You need to wipe your hand . . . after what just happened."

Chuckling softly he says, "Hold the wheel for a second and I'll take care of it."

The Tesla drives so smoothly that it's almost like I don't even need to hold it at all. Retaking the wheel, Exton gives me a quick smile before turning his full attention back to the freeway. I get lost in thought as I play the memory of what just happened over in my head. I can hardly believe any of that just happened to me, the most boring girl on earth.

"We're here, Beautiful. Don't open the door; I'll come around for you. Remember to breathe—there are photographers here."

I startle at his words because I was so deep in thought that I completely forgot we were still driving. Getting myself together, I smile as he opens the door and holds his hand out to me. Stepping from the car, I naturally lean into him when he puts his arm around my waist.

The flashing of the cameras going off is blinding and I worry about my ability to see enough to walk. I hesitate for a second before realizing that I just need to let Exton guide me. According to him the press expected here tonight was a "small" group. I'd guess it's probably less than twenty but it feels like a thousand.

The loud questions and directions to look a certain way are overwhelming.

"X! X! Who's your lady?"

"Exton, look this way!"

"Has this one seen your sex tape?"

Some of the questions are shouted at me.

"What's it like being with Triple X?"

"Who are you?"

"Look this way!"

Stopping near the door, Exton holds me close. Leaning into me he puts his mouth next to my ear. Under his breath he says, "Smile and let them have their pictures for the next minute. Then we can go in.""

Lifting his head he starts talking to the photographers. "Alright everyone, calm down. I'm here tonight to support Laz's opening and I want to focus on that."

They continue with their questions but he completely ignores them. It's like what I would imagine walking the gauntlet would be like, and I'm thrilled when he turns and guides me so that we walk into the restaurant.

Blinking away the flashes that I'm still seeing even though no more cameras are going off, I lean into Exton for support when I see all the people in the room. There's most of the cast of the cooking show that Laz was on, all of the Renegade Saints, the entire Hart family are all here, and there are several well-known actors and a bunch of reality TV stars.

Sliding his hand down to mine, Exton links our fingers together and then gently gives mine a squeeze. It's the littlest thing, but it makes me feel not so overwhelmed. Mentally shaking off my nerves, I squeeze back.

I can do this.

chapter eight

AFTER ABOUT HALF AN hour of circulating and meeting people, I'm significantly less nervous. Exton's been working the room and making sure to greet everyone, but now that's finished and he's in deep conversation with Gavin Wilde from the Renegade Saints about being the musical advisor for the show that Exton is writing.

I don't want to be the annoying kind of woman that hangs onto a man like he's a human life raft, so I start to pull my hand out of Exton's grip so that I can walk away and leave them to talk business. Instead of letting go, he holds on tighter. Looking at me, he shakes his head once in the negative before turning back to Gavin.

"I'll shoot you an email this week and we'll meet up to discuss it in more depth," he tells Gavin. If you'll excuse us, I need to go check in with Laz."

After Gavin walks away, Exton turns to me. "Is everything okay?"

"Everything's fine, I was just going to give you some breathing room. You shouldn't feel like you need to babysit me—"

Without a word, Exton starts walking us through the crowd. People say things and try to engage him, but he just smiles and keeps right on going until we enter the kitchen, which he strolls through until we reach another set of kitchen doors. When he walks us through, we're in a darkened hallway of what looks like the restaurant's office space. Turning right, he walks us down the hall before opening a door and bringing me into what is obviously Laz's office.

Once he shuts the door he positions me so that my back is against it. Setting a hand on either side of me, he glares down at me. "What the fuck was that about?" he asks briskly.

Licking my lips nervously, I look down. "I don't want to be a—"

"Stop," he commands firmly. "Whatever the hell you were about to say, just don't do it. I brought you here tonight because I want to be with you. I always want to be with you, but you continuously keep finding imaginary roadblocks. You're fucking mine and I want you next to me, Beautiful. Stop with the running."

I hate myself for feeling all shivery inside at his pronouncement that I'm his. Possessive Exton is hotter than ever and I am appalled by how turned on I am by his Alpha tendencies. What am I, a fifties housewife? Hell no! I need to put a stop to this right now before I make an even bigger fool out of myself.

Lifting my arms up, I cross them over my chest and glare at him. "You make it sound like I'm a puppy or some kind of property and that's disgusting. You aren't my owner, Exton!"

Placing a hand on either side of my waist he holds me still as he leans forward so that he's right up against me.

"Don't give me some bullshit about being property, because I *never* said that. What I said was the straight truth—you're mine. For the record, I'm just as much yours and you won't ever find me complaining about that."

I don't know what to say to that and the way it makes me feel is scary. I don't want to hope for things that aren't really possible. He's mine for right now, while it suits *him,* but I don't really believe that anything serious will come of it.

"The way that you twist things inside your head fucking kills me," he growls. "You have *no* reason to doubt anything about what's happening here, but I can tell just from the look on your face that you're grinding your gears and working overtime to make yourself believe that this is going to go bad. Stop putting so much energy into a false negative and focus on what's really happening."

He's right; I do look for the negative. I hate that I'm like this, but

strictly temporary

I'm scared. Blowing out a sigh of surrender, I nod my head. "I'll try harder."

"Good, because I'm not fucking going anywhere."

He gives me no chance to respond to that. I barely have time to process what he's said before he's kissing me. The kiss is hard and possessive, and I instinctively understand that he's dominating me and staking his claim. Gripping his shoulders, I kiss him back just as aggressively. The little growl that he lets out as he thrusts against me causes me to tear my mouth from his in order to let out a gasp.

Sliding his hands into my hair, he pushes it back as he tilts my head to the side. He starts ever so gently kissing my neck before trailing little love bites from just under my ear down to my collarbone. I let out a strangled sound of pure arousal when he sucks at a particularly tender spot, and I clench my inner muscles so hard that I just about come.

Lifting his head, he looks down into my eyes and lets out a groan. "You're so fucking sexy, Arden. How can you be so oblivious about what you do to me?"

Instead of waiting for me to answer—not that I've got anything coherent to say, mind you—he begins straightening my hair and my dress. When he's satisfied that I'm okay, he drops one last soft kiss on my lips before taking my hand and leading us back to the party.

***

The rest of the evening has been phenomenal. Everyone loved Laz's food and the atmosphere is really enjoyable. It's kind of funny that I was so nervous about coming when it's turned out to be much less intimidating than I had imagined. Now the night's drawing to a close and Exton is just waiting for a text from the valet alerting him that his car is at the front.

I'm not looking forward to going through the groups of photographers again, but there are worse things to have to deal with.

"Car's ready, baby. Let's go."

After saying our final goodbyes we head for Exton's car hand in hand. The second the door to the restaurant swings open for us to step out, the camera flashes start going off and questions are shouted.

"Exton! Exton! Look over here!"

"Tell us who you're with!"

"Who are you?"

"Look this way!"

Coming to a halt, Exton squeezes my hand as he faces the photographers.

"Come on guys," he laughs affably. "No need to yell at my girlfriend—"

The very instant the word girlfriend leaves his lips, they go from just interested to rabidly obsessed with getting details. If I thought the flashes and questions were overwhelming before, I had no clue. Now they're all yelling over each other and all I can really hear is "Girlfriend," over and over again.

Honestly, they're as shocked as I am. Who said anything about being his girlfriend? We never discussed that at all! I can tell that he's very aware of the fact that I've gone rigid. Seeming to realize that I'm completely overwhelmed, he squeezes my hand tighter and starts leading me through the small crowd that is now jostling us as they yell their questions.

Either he senses that I'm completely overwhelmed or he's just over their questions coming so fast and furious, because he's now hustling me through the crowd toward the car. Once he's sure that I'm safely seated, he hustles around the front of the car and gets into the driver's seat. In seconds he's got his seatbelt on and we're driving away from the restaurant.

My palms are now clammy and my heart is racing. Girlfriend? Who said anything about being his girlfriend? When this blows up I'm going to be nothing but a joke. I'll be like one of George Clooney's old girlfriends. Oh my God, what the heck did I get myself into by agreeing to be seen in public with him? This is a nightmare!

"Arden, don't—"

"Don't *what*, Exton? *Don't* have a reaction to the fact that you just threw me to the wolves? *Don't* get upset that they're going to dig until they find out who I am? *Don't* feel sick to my stomach because I'm going to look like the world's stupidest woman in front of thousands of people that I don't know? Which thing are you telling me *not* to do?"

Reaching out, he sets his hand on my knee. "Baby, none of that is true—"

"Screw your true, Exton! We are done. *D.O.N.E.* Done! You're an asshole and I can't believe that I was stupid enough to fall for your bullshit for even five goddamn seconds! You make me sick!" I shout angrily.

Letting go of my leg, Exton moves his hand to the steering wheel. Holding his hands at ten and two, he steers the car with a death grip without saying a word to me.

The longer that the silence stretches between us, the more panicked I get. I am beside myself about what just happened and I can't believe that there's any doubt in my mind that this needs to end tonight. I have to want to be done with him! Having questions thrown at me by the paparazzi is something that I have no interest in. I should be happy that he's not arguing any of this with me, glad that he's going to walk away without a backwards glance.

The silence in the car is almost deafening, and it's not helped along by the fact that since it's a Tesla, it's almost completely noiseless. The only thing that's filling the awkward quietness is the sound of our breathing.

Clenching my fists I hold myself stiff as I focus on how much longer I need to hold myself together. When I see the freeway exit for my neighborhood, I silently urge myself on. I can do this—it's only three or four more minutes, tops. Then I'll get out of the car and that will be that.

When he turns down my street, I take my seatbelt off. The second he stops the car at the curb, I throw the door open and jump out.

I snap out a harsh, "Have a nice life," as I slam the door behind me. Running up the walk, I burst into the courtyard of my building and haul ass up to my door. With trembling hands I open my clutch and pull my keys out, letting out a frustrated sound when my fingers don't cooperate as I try to fit the key into the lock. I need to keep myself together because I really don't want to have an emotional breakdown out here where any of my neighbors might see.

I startle when a hand covers mine. The only reason I don't scream at the top of my lungs is because a jolt of electricity zaps my hand the second he touches me, so I know that it's Exton. Looking over my shoulder at him I snap, "What're you doing?"

Taking the keys from my jelly-like fingers, he fits the correct one into the lock. "Unlocking the fucking door," he says tersely.

Turning the key, he flings the door open and guides me into the apartment. Spinning on my heel I immediately get angry when I see that he's locking the door behind him.

"I don't want you here," I say firmly. "I said everything that needed to be said in the car. What do you think you're doing by coming in here?"

He's turned away from me as he locks the door and throws the keys onto the table, but the second he turns back to me, I have no doubt about the fact that he's not happy.

"What am I doing? I'm fighting for you, goddammit! That shit you spouted in the car was ridiculous and I am *done* with you pushing me away like I'm some kind of fucking pariah! What have I done that makes you so motherfucking distrustful of me, Arden? Name one fucking thing!"

My fight or flight response has now kicked into full gear and I am desperate to run and hide. He has to go. "Are you really so cocky that you think that every woman alive will fall for your bullshit? You've fucked your way through the goddamn Victoria's Secret catalogue, you've got a sex tape and not two weeks before I met you, you took ten women home with you for an orgy! You just made me look like the stupidest woman alive in front of those photographers and by tomorrow afternoon I'll be the town joke!"

Letting out a harsh sound of pure frustration he runs a hand through his hair and closes his eyes. When he opens them, I find that they are blazing. "Are you fucking kidding me right now? You're throwing shit at me that isn't even true! Have I fucked models? Yes. Yes I have. I didn't give a baker's fuck about any of them and they didn't give a shit about me, Arden."

"I don't want to hear about—"

"No, that's not how this is going to work anymore! You threw this bullshit out, now I'm going to set your ass straight. You want to know how I feel about the fact that some goddamn cunt taped me during sex and then sold it to the highest bidder? I feel like a fucking idiot and there isn't a week that goes by that I don't think about it at some point. I didn't give permission for her to do that, I didn't know about it, and it fucking makes me sick. You have no fucking idea how badly that fucked with my head, or all the shit that I've done since then to make sure that nothing like that ever happens again."

"You don't know how much I hated myself for that one horrible judgment call. I should've known that she was out to fuck me over, but I didn't pay attention to the signs and it happened. I can't take it back. The only good thing I can say about that situation is that it's been a decade now. That stupid fucking Triple X name stuck, but almost no one posts screenshots or shit from the video anymore. You know the real me, Arden. Not Triple X. Not the fucking asshole who fucked off and made mistakes that can never be erased—but you won't admit that to yourself and I'm done letting you pretend that this isn't fucking real."

Seeing the pain on his face as he talks about the tape slices at my heart. I know how it feels to have someone play me for a fool in a way that can never be smoothed over. I will always carry the weight of what happened with Ricky, and I will always hate myself for being stupid enough to fall for his lies.

"I'm sorry," I tell him. "I shouldn't have brought that up. I never cared about the tape—"

"I'm not finished," he snaps. "That ridiculous fucking orgy story you just threw at me? Baby, you're about to find out that I can go all night long—but even I couldn't take on ten women and come out able to walk the next day. That story was fucking bullshit from beginning to goddamn end, as are most of the stories you see on the Internet or read in the gossip rags. I told you from the start that if you had any questions or concerns about any of the bullshit you read to tell me about it. Instead of addressing it head on, you said nothing."

"I didn't—"

"And then," he continues on as he ignores my attempt to speak, "You throw a goddamn hissy fit over the fact that I *accurately* said that you're my girlfriend. One of us here has been shooting straight this entire time, and it isn't you. I couldn't have made it any clearer that my intentions towards you are solid. You want to look me in the fucking eye and tell me that you're not my goddamn girlfriend and that you don't want to be? Because if you can do it, you aren't just scared, you're a fucking liar."

I'm grasping at straws trying to come up with an answer. Finally I go with the only thing I can think of.

"You never asked me to be your girlfriend," I answer hotly.

Throwing his hands in the air, he lets out a sound of pure frustration. "Am I here every day? Do I text, call and email you all day every day? Do I treat you like you're my goddamn Queen? I do *all* of that and you aren't paying attention if you think I'm not your boyfriend. I don't know what the fuck you're so afraid of, and I don't know why you want to work so hard to push me away when it's so obvious that what you really want is to be closer. The bottom line is that no matter what bullshit you throw out, it doesn't change the fact that I. Am. Your. Fucking. Boyfriend," he growls as he begins closing the distance between us.

chapter nine

I'M TOO SHOCKED BY the feral look in his eyes to move a muscle. When he stops in front of me he reaches out and fists one hand in my hair as the other settles on my ass. Pulling me in without a word, he covers my mouth with his own. There is no slow build up here. Instead he's clearly set out to conquer me, and I have no desire to fight. Whether I want to admit it to him, or even to myself, I care and deep down I want him to belong to me.

I startle when my back meets a wall, then let out a groan when he starts moving his hand up my thigh.

"I thought about fucking you against this wall all night," he says huskily.

Holy hell, I'm actually going to let him take me up against this wall.

Taking a breath for courage I nod and then blurt, "Then take me."

I expect him to come back to kissing me, but instead he bends a bit and lifts me up into his arms before he starts walking toward my bedroom. "I'll be damned if the first time we make love is in your goddamn hallway," he says. "I'm going to taste and explore every perfect inch of your body, and we need a bed for that."

When we get into my room he sets me down next to my bed. I shiver as he turns me around and runs his hands over the fabric of my dress until he finds the zipper on the side. As he pulls it down, I remember something important. Covering his hand, I let out a squeak. "Wait, don't!"

He stops immediately but then spins me to face him. "What's wrong?"

It's actually embarrassingly hilarious, and I can't help but laugh. I know that I am blushing furiously as I answer, "My boobs are taped into the dress. I just remembered that my skin could chafe off if you pulled the top down."

Throwing his head back, he lets out a laugh. "I will never understand why you women do the most painful shit to yourselves all in the name of fashion or beauty. You rip the hair out of your legs and tape your tits into dresses. If someone tried to wax my legs or tape my nuts down, I'd go ape shit."

I'm laughing as he grips my shoulders and guides me down so that I'm sitting on the bed. After turning on the bedside light he crouches down in front of me and runs his finger absently over my knee. "Is there a special technique for getting the tape off?"

"I'll just go into the bathroom and take care of it myself. You don't need to see that my boobs are quadruple taped into this dress. I know it's not attractive to have to see all the crap that went into getting this look" I say with a laugh.

Reaching, up he cups my chin. "Every part of you is beautiful," he says firmly, "And you never need to hide yourself from me. I see you, Arden, all of you. If you think a little tit tape is going to make me run, you're not paying attention. Now tell me, is there anything you need to get the tape off without hurting yourself?"

Swallowing nervously, I shake my head. "I don't think there's anything to use to make it come off easier, at least not that I've ever heard of. Normally I just need to pull it off slowly and hope that it's quick and painless."

He grimaces as he nods his head and watches silently as I reach up to my back and undo the clasp that held the top part of my dress up. I can feel his eyes on me as I slowly start peeling the top of my dress down. I work the left side and then the right, sending up a silent thank you to the boob tape gods that the tape is peeling off fairly easily. It takes a few minutes but eventually I get it to come off without having ripped or chaffed any of my skin.

It hits me that I'm about to be naked in front of him for the first time and I feel my heart rate pick up. My thought is that the best way to handle this is just to get it over with.

"I'm going to stand up and just take the dress off," I say shyly.

He growls as he stands up and looks down at me. "No, beautiful. I get to undress you."

Covering my hands with his, he clasps the fabric of my top between his fingers and starts pulling it down. When my breasts spill out, he lets out a choked sound that causes me to look up worriedly. I'm not sure what I expect to find, but my already hard nipples harden even more when I see the look of raging lust on his face.

"Jesus fuck," he rasps, "You're stunning, baby. I'm going to fuck those tits and then cover them with my come."

I let out a gasp at his words as a visual of what that would look like dances through my head.

Cupping my breasts in his hands, he rubs my nipples with his thumbs. "I want you to wear me and only me. I'm going to come on you everywhere," he tells me. "There is no part of you that I won't mark. You're mine, beautiful."

Looking into my eyes, he smiles. "Lie back so that we can get the rest of this off."

The way his eyes are devouring me and the look of reverence in them is making me dizzy, so lying down is probably a good idea. Doing as he instructs, I lay back and then lick my lips nervously when he grasps either side of my dress and starts pulling it down. I lift my hips automatically when I need to and he rewards me with a smile. Bringing my dress the rest of the way down my legs, he pulls it off and tosses it aside.

His eyes rake over me slowly, almost as if he's mapping every single inch of my skin. I can't help but feel self-conscious about what he's seeing. I'm not a model—I'm a normal woman with flaws. Shifting nervously, I gesture to the light. "Can you please turn that off?" I say shyly.

Eyes flying up to mine, he frowns. "Fuck no, woman! I'm never going to give up any chance to see you better. Baby, you're the most stunning woman I've ever set eyes on and I don't want to miss anything. I know what would make you feel better about having the lights on, though."

I raise my eyebrow in silent question and I open my mouth to ask him what he means at the same moment he pulls his suit jacket off. Reaching into the inner pocket, he pulls out a few gold foil packets and shows them to me before setting them on my bedside table and tossing his jacket to the floor. I feel myself blushing furiously as it dawns on me that if he hadn't thought to bring protection, this night would be ending quite abruptly when we got down to the most important part.

"I'll always take care of you," he says huskily.

"I can't believe you carried those around all night," I laugh nervously.

"I didn't and that's a good thing because if I had, things probably would've gotten out of control in Laz's office. I bought a box the other day and put it in my glove compartment tonight, just in case."

I'm more than thankful that he's on point, and I can now admit to myself that I would be heartbroken if we'd been unable to make love. I want this—badly.

I never knew that watching as a man undresses could be such a turn on, but as he takes off his tie and begins to unbutton his shirt, my core is clenching with need.

Sliding his shirt off, he tosses it in the same direction he dropped his jacket. My eyes travel over his torso hungrily as I eat up the visual before me. This man is beautiful and so sexy that I can barely stand it.

I gulp nervously as he undoes his belt buckle and slides the belt out of the loops of his pants. Stepping closer to me, he surprises me as he runs the end of the belt softly from my collarbone down to the center of my panties and then onto my knee. I let out a choked sound as goose bumps rise on my skin.

"So responsive," he says huskily.

After dropping the belt to the floor, he undoes the button of his pants and pulls the zipper down. There's something so arousing about watching him undress that I have trouble swallowing. As his pants hit the floor and he kicks them aside, I feel my pulse kick up to hyper speed. I watch silently as he removes his socks before standing up straight so that I can see him. All that's left covering him now is a pair of black Calvin Klein briefs and they aren't doing *anything* to conceal the fact that he's very aroused—and it looks like TMZ isn't kidding when they refer to him as the writer with the big package.

Climbing onto the bed with me, he pulls me into his arms and immediately starts kissing me again. My body has a mind of its own as my legs spread wide and wrap around his waist while my fingers slide into his hair. He rubs himself against my soaked panties with a growl, and I let out a little mew of pleasure as I feel myself getting even wetter. He feels amazing on top of me, and I am incredibly turned on by being skin on skin with him almost entirely.

He kisses me passionately, both of us moaning at different times as we rub against each other. Cupping my ass in his hands, he takes control of moving me up and down against his hardness.

After ending our kiss, he slowly starts licking and biting a trail down my neck and collarbone to my right breast. His tongue laps at my skin greedily as I shift beneath him desperately in an attempt to get some relief. His tongue explores every inch of my breast—except my nipple, and I can barely contain my shock when I hear myself begging him to suck it.

"Use your tongue on it," I beg brokenly. "I want to feel you."

He complies and sucks my nipple into his mouth as he swirls his tongue over it again and again. Tilting my head back, I let out a silent scream.

When he starts trailing kisses over to my left breast I quiver with anticipation. I never knew that it could feel like this, never knew that I could want someone this much.

"These fucking tits," he chokes out. "So perfect."

He worships them with his tongue, teeth, lips and fingers as I write beneath him in exquisite agony. Lifting his head he says, "As good as your tits taste, I know that I'm never going to get enough of the taste of your pussy. The way your honey melted on my tongue in the car almost made me come in my pants like a damn teenager. One hit and I'm already an addict for it—and now I'm going to get it right from the source."

I quiver when he slides a hand between us, trailing it down my stomach. Cupping his hand against my panty-covered mound, he lets out a groan. "I can feel your heat, beautiful. You're so ready for me to take control and make you come again. Remembering the way you squeezed my fingers earlier is making my dick so goddamn hard."

Gripping either side of my underwear in his hands he slides them down my legs. I groan when I glance down and see the look of pure lust on his face as he settles onto the bed. He spreads my legs with his shoulders as he stares down at my drenched sex.

"Christ, Arden," he moans. "You've got the most beautiful cunt. Every damn inch of you is so fucking perfect."

When he leans in and settles his nose against my mound, I forget to breathe.

"Mine," he says rumbles from somewhere deep down in his throat.

Opening his mouth he blows softly up toward the top of my mound before rubbing his nose just above my throbbing clit. I'm unable to hold in my squeak of surprise and when he chuckles in response I both hear it and feel the vibration between my legs.

Before I can even take a breath, he begins gently rolling his tongue from my channel to my clit, back and forth. Of their own accord, my hands are now fisted in the sheet below me. Unable to hold still, I rock against his tongue as he continues his exploration.

"Oh," I gasp as he adjusts position, lifting me up more and spreading my legs wider so that I'm more open to him. Stars appear behind my eyelids as he begins sliding his tongue in and out of my soaking pussy. I groan in annoyance when he removes the tongue, but the groan quickly changes to one of pleasure as he replaces it with a finger.

His tongue works my clit as his finger glides in and out and I can feel my juices mixing with his saliva to make me wetter. Briefly I wonder if I'm embarrassing myself by being this wet, but the growls and moans he's letting out make it clear that he's enjoying it all.

I thrill at the pornographic sound of him lapping at my super-sensitive clit. The sound of my own cries startles me because it's never happened for me like this before. I'm a panting, moaning, ball of need and it's all because of him.

"I love eating your pussy," he growls. "I don't want you wearing panties when we're together ever again," he says as his finger starts working inside of me faster. "I need access, beautiful. Anywhere, anytime, I need to be able to get to this sweet cunt and feast. Promise me, baby. No more panties."

My head thrashes from side to side as I feel him making a come hither motion inside of me. I know he wants an answer but I'm too gone to form words. Reaching down I fist my hand in his hair and thrust against his face.

"Such a greedy pussy," he says huskily as he fights the pressure and lifts his head. "But I'm not making you come until you tell me that this pussy belongs to me and you'll let me have you as many times a day as I need you."

"Yes, yes," I chant my agreement as my hips roll and I try to get his mouth back on me.

"Yes, this pussy is mine?"

"Yes!"

"Any time I need my fix you'll let me in?"

I can't answer because he's added another finger and he's scissoring them inside of me.

"Look at me," he commands as he stops moving his fingers.

Lifting my head, I look down at him frantically.

"I want you with me, Arden. No more fucking running. You're mine. This pussy is mine. Everything you have to give, I'm taking. I want it all. That means no more bullshit about who you belong to, and you accept that this is a real relationship. Do you admit it?"

It's a weird thing to be looking between my legs, seeing his face and understanding that he's serious. The truth is that he wouldn't be here and I wouldn't have let him do any of this if I weren't just as invested in him. Everything I've been telling myself about keeping a wall up has been nothing but bullshit.

"Yes," I answer firmly. "I admit it."

His relieved, "Finally," melts my insides. After smiling at me he turns his attention back to my pussy. Immediately, his fingers start pumping in and out again and his tongue goes back to slow and steady licks.

Within two minutes I'm out of breath and frantically thrusting against his face as I feel my release bearing down on me. As he hones in on the top of my clit and sucks steadily, I burst into flames with a loud cry as my body shakes through my orgasm.

I assume that he'll stop licking me and start fucking me now, but he doesn't. Instead he spreads my pussy lips with his fingers and goes right back to making me crazy. I'm so sensitive from my orgasm that I can't contain the whiny little, "Nooo," that I let out. "I can't come like that again," I whimper.

Raising his head, he looks me in the eye and then licks his lips. "You're going to come all over my tongue again, baby. When you're finished shaking and screaming, I'm going to fill you with my cock and fuck you until you can't feel anything but me for days. You'll come again with me deep inside of you and when you can't take it anymore, I'm going to pull out and come on you. No spot that I won't mark, baby, remember?"

"Uh-huh," I squeak in the form of an answer.

What was I saying about not being able to come again? If he just keeps up the dirty talk I'll come from that alone.

He's more aggressive with his tongue now, exploring every last bit of me as his fingers begin thrusting faster and harder. Arching my back, I yell out as he starts rubbing that perfect spot inside of me.

"Oh God, Exton! Right there, right there, *right there!* Fuck!"

I come apart with a hoarse cry as my pussy clenches and unclenches against his fingers. I moan when he removes his fingers, my body still reeling with aftershocks. The sound of a foil wrapper tearing brings me back from my cloud and I sit up fast to see.

When I see his cock at attention in front of me, I lose my breath. Jesus, he's hard, huge and glorious. Licking my lips, I stare at the head with fascination. I've never given a blowjob before but right now the only thing going through my head is my inner voice screaming *I want that* over and over. When my hand reaches out and grips his shaft, he and I both gasp at the same time.

It's hot in my hand, and the choked groan that Exton lets out emboldens me. Leaning forward I stick out my tongue and circle the tip, letting out a moan of pleasure as his flavor spreads across my tongue. I never imagined myself caring about a man's dick being near my mouth, but right now I want to make a meal of Exton Alexander's perfect cock.

Opening my mouth, I suck the head in, wetting it with plenty of my saliva for lubrication. I tread carefully because I've never done this before, but now I want as much of his cock in my mouth as possible. He lets me explore, encouraging me with his sexy but ridiculously filthy words.

"Fuck baby, you look so fucking good with my cock in your

mouth."

And then, "Yeah, such a good little cocksucker. Just like that, Beautiful."

The more he reacts, the more confident I feel. I open my mouth wide as I suck and work on his shaft, desperate to get him as deep in my mouth as possible. When I finally get his tip to hit the back of my throat I let out an involuntary gurgling noise and immediately pull off in embarrassment.

"Oh fuck, Arden," he growls. "That fucking noise. I almost just came down your perfect throat."

Looking up at him in surprise I ask, "Really?"

"Yes," he says firmly. "I loved that fucking sound and I plan to enjoy it over and over again."

Now I feel like a million bucks, so I lean in to take him back into my mouth. Setting his hands on my shoulders, Exton keeps me from moving.

"It's time to get off your knees and get up onto the bed. As badly as I want you sucking my dick, I need to be in your pussy more. I need to fuck you."

Even at a moment like this, he's still a gentleman. Helping me up onto the bed, he gets me situated before he grabs the condom wrapper he already started to open and pulls it out. I watch, fascinated, as he sheaths himself. Seeing it like this I almost can't believe I just had that thing in my mouth—he's huge. For the first time, I have feelings of panic as I wonder if he'll fit inside of me without pain.

Climbing onto the bed, he settles on top of me, his cock resting against my soaked mound. Rubbing back and forth, he murmurs something I don't quite catch before covering my mouth with his and kissing me. My arms wrap around him and hold on tight as he thrusts against me and kisses me deeply, our tongues locked in a sexual duel that I know is going to end with amazing orgasms for us both.

Lifting his head, he stares down at me with the sexiest look I've ever seen. "Now," he says, "I'm going to fuck you until you scream for me. Spread wide, baby. I'm going deep."

When I feel him position himself at my entrance, all of my breath leaves me in a whoosh. Holding himself up with one arm, he uses the other to rub my clit as he slowly begins sliding inside of me, one incredible inch at a time.

I struggle to remember to breathe as my pussy adjusts to his girth and lets him in. I'm so full of him that I swear I can feel him in every cell of my body.

"So fucking tight," he moans brokenly. "You're everything, Arden. You're so fucking perfect, so fucking mine."

I let out a yell of wonder when I feel him sink all the way in, and my thighs clamp tightly at his sides as he tries to pull back. "No," I whimper. "Stay inside of me. Just like this—always like this."

Setting his forehead against mine he rasps, "Open your eyes. I need to see you."

As soon as I do, I find myself lost in the cognac colored ecstasy of his gaze.

"That's right, eyes on me. I fucking love when you look at me."

I tighten around him as my pussy responds to his words and the heat of his gaze.

"I need to move now, Beautiful. Let me love you."

Nodding my head in understanding, I let out a sharp sound of wonder as he pulls out halfway and then thrusts back in. My body surprises me by naturally knowing what to do even though I have no real experience. I meet him thrust for thrust as he powers into me, his cock hitting me just right on every forward stroke.

When he picks up speed and hits me deeper, I scream out his name.

"Yes," he growls. "Fuck yes. Scream for me, Arden. Yell my fucking name!"

The harder he fucks me, the louder I yell. His balls slap against my ass over and over again as the mattress groans beneath us. Kissing me deep and hard, he starts thrusting faster and really pounding against me. I'm aware that I'm scratching his back, but I don't care because I can't stop.

When he pinches my clit between his fingers, I break the kiss and come with a scream. I'm still coming as he flips me over and maneuvers me onto my knees before slamming back inside of me. I call his name again and again as he fucks into me.

"Your tight cunt feels so good," he says breathlessly from behind me.

Grabbing the iron bars of my bed, I push back to meet him thrust for thrust. If he wanted to stake his claim on me, he's done it because in this moment I understand that I'll never be the same.

Reaching around, he slides his hand between my legs and begins rubbing circles on my clit. "Come on my dick, Arden. Show me how much you love letting me in so deep."

"Exton," I cry. "Fuck me!"

"Always, beautiful. Always."

As my orgasm breaks over me, I arch my back and silently scream as my entire body shakes. He keeps right on going, pulling every last possible bit of my orgasm out. By the time it's done, I'm dripping with sweat and completely overwhelmed.

Pulling out of me he says, "Turn over."

As soon as I do and he has me where he wants me, he rips the condom off and starts jerking his cock. "You're fucking incredible," he pants as he strokes hard and fast. "Never felt like this, never knew—"

When I lift my head and touch the head of his cock with my finger, he lets out an animalistic sound of pleasure and starts coming hotly against my stomach. "Fuck, Arden, fuck! Yes, fuck . . . yes."

I never would've thought that watching a man come on me would be sexy. Not only is it sexy, it's intimate. He was right, I feel marked.

Dropping onto the bed beside me, he kisses me gently as he rubs his come around on my skin.

Breaking the kiss, he adjusts us so that he's holding me in his arms. Looking down into my eyes, he smiles.

"I love you wearing me," he says possessively.

I'm so orgasm dumb that I can't even respond with a coherent sentence. Instead I chuckle softly and curl into him. Within seconds I feel my eyes drifting shut and I enjoy my last few seconds of being awake as his fingers trail over my skin.

chapter ten

LETTING MYSELF INTO EXTON'S house, I let out a sigh of pleasure as I kick my shoes off and carry my overnight bag up to the bedroom to change into some casual clothes. It took about a week after we made love for the first time for him to talk me into spending time at his house. I was uncomfortable at first, but now I'm okay. As the weeks go by we get closer and more of my walls start to come down. I'm still scared—not terrified anymore, but there is still fear that something bad could happen—but I'm getting used to being his girlfriend.

It helped that the morning after we made love, Exton got on the phone with his publicist and composed a press release to confirm his relationship status. There was a lot of interest in the fact that he's dating a working girl and there were a few paparazzi at my car each day for about two weeks, but now it's died down and we're old news.

After changing out of my work clothes I head toward Exton's office to tell him that I'm home. He's been hard at work on his script and he likes to stay in what he calls his writing cave until the minute I'm home.

I can't help but smile when I hear his voice, but it quickly falls away when I hear what he's saying.

"No goddammit, you find me a way to get in touch with whoever the fuck this Ricky Greenway is and I'm gonna find it now! I can't have naked pictures of my girlfriend on the Internet goddammit! How many pictures were there and what was the sale price? I'll double it—fuck, I'll quadruple it!"

My hand flies to my mouth as all of the breath leaves my body. *What naked pictures?*

It takes a minute for me to realize that Exton is now yelling. "No! I refuse to believe that it's too late to get them back! You're not understanding what the fuck I'm saying right now—I cannot fucking deal with this shit!"

Oh my God. Why? How is this happening?

As Exton continues yelling, my brain starts running a million miles an hour and I can only focus on one thing. He doesn't want to deal with this—and I don't want him to have to tell me that to my face.

Turning on my heel, I run down the hall, grab my purse and slip back into my work shoes. I look like an idiot in yoga pants, a tank top and high heels, but I don't care. I run to my car at top speed and within seconds I'm peeling out of Exton's driveway.

Home, I just need to be home.

I break a land speed record to get to my apartment, and I completely ignore my cell phone as it rings practically non-stop the entire time. Turning onto my street, I stop with a screech of tires when I see a few paparazzi gathering outside my apartment building.

What this means hits me like a kick to the stomach as I stare at the assembling mass—there really are pictures, and they really are going to be all over the Internet. I'm ruined. Everyone is going to see me naked and everyone is going to know that I was married to someone who took my virginity for a bet. The humiliation of everyone knowing is going to destroy me.

Backing up, I drive a few blocks over before pulling into an alley and stopping my car. Picking up my cell, I find the screen full of missed calls from Exton. I'm shaking so hard I can barely hold the phone.

What the hell am I going to do?

It takes me a few minutes to stop shaking enough to form a coherent thought, all the while ignoring the ringing of my cell phone. Finally, I realize that there's only one person who I trust to give me advice. Picking up the phone, I scroll through my contacts and then hit call.

As soon as she picks up, I start crying.
"Sabrina, I need your help."

acknowledgements

I'd like to thank the wonderful bloggers, readers, authors, cover designers, formatters and editors that I've met since I became an Author. This is a wonderful job that I'm very aware that I'm blessed to have. I never lose sight of that.

strictly temporary
volume two

USA Today Bestselling Author
ELLA FOX

dedication

This book is for everyone that had to pick themselves up and start anew. You're braver than you know.

"Once in a while, right in the middle of an ordinary life, love gives us a fairy tale."—Anonymous

prologue

TWO THINGS WAKE ME up—the fact that my head is pounding and the need to piss. It takes a bit of time for me to be alert enough to understand that the noise isn't just in my head—it's the sound of someone pounding on my front door.

Scrambling out of the bed, I groggily curse the assholes who are damn near breaking my front door down with their banging. Deciding that taking a piss takes precedence, I make a pit stop in my bathroom and quickly take care of business before making my way down to my front door.

Flinging the door open as I let out a string of expletives, I'm in no way surprised to find my two best friends, Lazarus and Dante, on the other side. These fuckers have done this to me a few times over the years—waking me up like assholes and then laughing at me when they tell me to get dressed to go somewhere. The last time they pulled this, we wound up in Miami for a two-day beach party that I'm fairly sure I'm still hung over from.

"You've got to stop this shit, assholes. You know I hate being woken up like—"

My words come to a halt when I realize that there are dozens of photographers on the sidewalk behind them. The click-click-click of the cameras is loud as fuck when there are so many going off at the same time. It's loud enough that I can hear it even over the gibberish that's being yelled out. The shit they're yelling—one on top of the other—makes no fucking sense.

"Like a fucking hurricane—"

"What brand of condom—"

"Is she your girlfriend—"

"Everyone is going to see—"

"You're my hero!"

I'm completely baffled by what's happening and have no idea what the hell to do or say. Without a word, Dante and Laz shove past me, coming into the house. Slamming the door behind him, Laz looks at me wide-eyed. "Dude, this is fucking bad."

Shaking my head in the hopes of clearing it I ask, "What the fuck is happening out there?"

"You need to sit down," Dante says.

He says it calmly, but I can tell that he's on edge about something. It's clear that they both are.

I follow Laz into my den, dropping onto the couch without a word as I wait for one of them to tell me what the fuck is going on.

"First of all, you need to either start charging your fucking cell phone in your damn bedroom at night or you need to put a fucking telephone in there. It would've helped to be able to call you," Dante says firmly. He's always been the dad of our group. He seems to come by it naturally.

"Phone. Bedroom. Check," I respond as I nod my agreement. "Now can you tell me what the fuck is going on?"

"This is bad," Laz says. "There's no way to tell you this that's going to make it okay, so I'm just going to say it. Some bitch sold a tape she made of the two of you having sex. It's fucking everywhere—and I do mean everywhere. It's all over the Internet, and it was on the fucking news this morning. When your manager couldn't get a hold of you, he called me. I got Dante on the phone—luckily *he* keeps a phone in his bedroom like a normal person—and we got here as quickly as we could."

I stare at him in horrified confusion. This can't be real—it's a mistake. Looking back and forth between the two of them, I find that they're both looking very solemn and serious. Fuck—this isn't a joke.

"That's bullshit," I respond firmly. "I didn't make a sex tape. I would never do that. Come on, man—"

"No, you didn't," Dante says. "But whoever you were with, did. Your manager told Laz the chick's name is Candy Lanz. I think it's safe to assume that's a fake fucking name—"

There's actual pain as I force myself to swallow past the bile that's creeping up my throat. I know exactly who he's talking about.

"Fuck," I say in a pained voice. "I should've fucking gone with my first goddamn instinct. I kept running into Candy at clubs. She seemed tough, you know? I knew shit was off, but one night I got stuck talking to her she gave me a whole story about walking in on her fiancée having sex with her best friend—who was a dude. I felt bad for her, so I started being nice."

"She kissed me, and I tried to say no . . . but she started crying and said she needed to have sex again. She gave me this whole sad story about how she needed to know that she was still attractive in order to move on from her ex. I felt like there was no harm in helping her feel that everything was going to be okay . . . You know how it is. I thought it was just going to be a simple fuck."

Shaking my head in frustration, I struggle to remain calm as it dawns on me what a duplicitous bitch Candy is. She clearly had a plan in order to have had cameras on hand.

"I went home with her one night about a month ago, fucked her and then quickly rolled, just like normal. I was relieved when I never heard another word from her, because the sex was uncomfortable as fuck. It was like she was working from a porn star's handbook, and I just wanted it to be over."

Standing from the couch, I start pacing the room. Like most people, my knowledge of sex tapes is limited to Rob Lowe's snafu and the infamous Tommy Lee and Pamela Anderson sex tape. What I know for sure is that this shit can't be legal.

"I need to lawyer up," I say firmly. "I want the strongest, most kick-ass attorney in the country to get on this. I want this fucking shit to be a distant memory ASAP. I'll bankrupt myself to get this thing off the Internet."

Rising from the easy chair he's sitting on, Laz comes my way and claps his hand on my shoulder. "We're behind you a hundred percent.

Let's find you a lawyer and get this shit into the rearview mirror."

I have to believe that this can be dealt with. The alternative—the potential of thousands of strangers seeing me having sex—is too awful to consider.

chapter one

Exton

WITH BEER IN HAND and a smile on my face, I watch as my friend's two sons attempt to teach their little sister how to play with the enormous inflatable bowling set I brought for them. Since Dante had his kids, and I became an honorary uncle, I've always made it a point to come back from my trips with a fun toy—or several. He tells me I spoil the kids terribly, but that's what being the cool honorary uncle is all about.

Up until Dante had kids, I never even imagined being a dad, but when I'm around them sometimes I wonder what it might be like to have a family. It'd be great to have kids, but I haven't met a woman I could spend two weeks with; much less fifty years. According to Dante, I just need to find a woman that makes me feel "The Spark."

The first time he said that shit to me, I about died laughing. The Spark? To me, that sounds like some crazy shit and, honestly, I don't buy that it happens for many people. I think it probably exists for a few, but definitely not for everyone. Dante is a lucky son-of-a-bitch, I'll say that. He wasn't even looking—his wife, Sabrina, just appeared one day and that was that.

Rina's the full package—beautiful, smart, and one of the nicest people I've ever met. Add to that the fact that she's an amazing mother, and I have to admit, I may have a bit of envy for what Dante has found. It's funny that back in college he was so anti-relationship, he swore at least a million times that he'd never have kids.

Watching him with his brood always makes me wonder what kind of father I'd make if I ever get the chance. I'm a big believer in the theory that you learn what you live. My father is not what you would call a parent. I simply refer to him as Joe, not Dad, and I haven't spoken to him in years. Joe's all about himself and what will benefit him the most—which is not conducive to good parenting.

I was pretty much born knowing that I wanted to write stories, but Joe never accepted that as a viable career choice. He was an actor when he met my mom, and she'd supported him for a lot of years while he played the audition game. Big breaks tended to come in the form of commercials that meant residual checks would roll in, but his career never took off.

I'd never even thought about acting—not even for a minute. It wasn't even on my radar at all. At least not until my dad started reading up on what was happening with Macauley Culkin, and then he decided that I was going to be a star. Overnight I went from being an eleven-year-old kid screwing around with my friends and writing short stories to being overwhelmed with acting classes, headshots, auditions and reading lines.

The truth is that I sucked as an actor. The shitty thing was that not everyone agreed, and I wound up doing a teen romantic comedy that was a huge hit. There are laws and shit in place to stop parents from stealing money from their children—but it didn't matter. My dad called himself my manager and took almost sixty percent. He was living the dream while I got stuck in a nightmare. I was on the cover of teen magazines and when I tried to go out and be normal people screamed in my face and made a huge deal out of me. It was fucking embarrassing and hard to deal with, especially at that age.

My father subscribed to the churn and burn method of management, and in six years I made fourteen films. I think one of them is halfway decent—the others are just humiliating. When I turned eighteen and had control of my life, I told my father to back the fuck off, and I went to college. It takes a special kind of asshole to be against their child getting an education, and Joe Alexander was that guy. He was furious with me, and I had to hear daily rants about what a fucking idiot I was.

He stuck around for another year in the hopes that I'd change my mind, but when I didn't, we had a massive blowout. Now he only gets in touch when he wants cash, tickets to a premiere, or to pretend that he wants to be a pal. I ignore that shit entirely.

"Smells like something's burning over here."

Pulled from my thoughts about shitty parents, I turn to Dante in confusion. "I don't smell anything."

Taking a swig of his beer, he laughs. "I was talking about your brain, dickhead. It looked like you were over here figuring out the path to world peace."

I know he wouldn't be cursing if the kids could hear us, but I still look over his shoulder just to be sure. A few months ago I was over here shooting the shit with Dante. He had been trying to set me up with some girl, and I'd gotten annoyed and had called him a jackass. His daughter Vivi spent the next week saying the word whenever she could.

I don't want to be that uncle, so I make every attempt to reel in my bad language when I'm around the kids. Vivi has a bad case of monkey see, monkey do when I'm around, so I'm always on the lookout for her. She also has a tendency just to appear, so it's always best to be careful. After making sure that she's still occupied with her brothers, I flip him off.

"Shut up, fucker. I was just thinking about how the restaurant is coming along. You still think we'll get it open on schedule?"

"I'm not going to lie—it's going to be tough. Not so much the construction part as the licenses, particularly the liquor license. That shit is taking forever. But I feel confident that we'll be able to push through and get Laz's up and open on time."

Rubbing at the back of my neck, I let out a sound of frustration. "Hopefully it will help get Laz out of this . . . funk. Ever since he got home from filming Chef-Tacular, and all that shit went down with Lindy, he's been a mess. It's been a year and he still hasn't been able to get himself together."

"Yeah, I hear you. At this point, I'm just glad to see him up and around again. What she did was fucked up, no doubt about it, but he's got to move on. I'm not trying to be a dick; I just hate to see how badly it's all fucked with his mind."

Drinking a bit of my beer, I nod. "If we ever see that crazy bitch again, I'm personally going to pay Sabrina to beat her ass. We can't touch her, but fuck does she need to be smacked down."

That makes him laugh. "I agree that she needs to be smacked, but you and I both know I'd freak the fuck out if Sabrina were in a situation where she could be hurt."

Rolling my eyes, I shake my head. "Dude, you're beyond whipped. Sometimes I look at you like this and I think—what the fuck happened to the guy that used to tell women straight up that if they got attached, they were out? I believe your exact words were that you'd rather chew off your left arm than get married. Now look at you."

We joke about this a lot, so I know that what I've said won't upset him at all. Instead, he laughs. "I told you, man. When you meet the one and you feel the spark, that's it. Game over. I was so set on staying single, but I'm happier than I ever imagined I could be with Sabrina and our kids. Even thinking about how empty my life would be without them makes me sick. Someday you'll know exactly what I'm talking about."

"How many times do I have to tell you—"

"Don't start that shit where you tell me not everyone gets this lucky. According to my wife, you're one of the good guys, and you need to find your woman ASAP. Not to get all emo on you or anything, but I agree. You haven't trusted anyone since that shit with the sex tape happened. You don't date, and you keep a separate fuck pad so that chicks don't know where you live. Look, I've been there. I didn't want shit in my home either—but your issues go a lot deeper because of that damn tape."

"So I've got issues now?" I question with a laugh.

"I'm not saying you're defective or anything. I'm just saying that other than my family, you haven't been able to let your guard down with anyone that you didn't know prior to the tape since it happened. You're right to be cautious—that shit was fucked up, and it shouldn't have happened. But not everyone is like that skank. All I'm saying is, don't be so uptight that when you do meet someone you wind up blowing it because of your trust issues."

"I promise that if I meet someone that makes me feel anything stronger than a simple erection, I'll work on keeping my issues in check, Doctor Hart."

"You need to let me set you up with this—'"

Holding up a hand, I stop him. "Fuck to the no, man. I don't date. You know this. I figure if I meet someone I'm genuinely interested in knowing, I'll date then. But you setting me up would be a fucking nightmare. This is the second time you've tried in the last year. Please tell me that you're not trying to set me up with everyone that you know who's still single. Fuck, do you do this shit to Laz?"

"No," he says through a laugh. "I don't fucking do it to Laz, because I don't know anyone I think would be a good fit. I'm not trying to set you up with just anyone, alright? Rina has gotten close with this girl, and I'm telling you, I think you'd like her."

Raising an eyebrow at him, I can't help but wonder if being married turns you into a couples-only zombie who believes that *Everyone. Must. Mate.* Dante isn't what you would call Mr. Cupid, so I've got to think he's just taking a stab in the dark here in the hopes that Sabrina's single friend can date one of his single friends.

Jesus. What a nightmare.

"Is this really what marriage has made of you? Are you going to be that guy now? Dude. I'm single, and I gotta say, it isn't a bad life."

"I didn't say it was a bad life—but I know from experience that it can be better. Don't be an ass about this—I'm trying to help. I would never try to set you up if I didn't have a strong feeling about it."

Huh. Maybe he is serious. "Alright, you've got me curious. Tell me about her—what's she look like?"

"That *would* be your first question, asshole. She's about Sabrina's height, and she's got long dark hair—"

I stop him right there, by making a buzzer noise. "Nope. I like blondes and redheads. You know that."

"Don't be a dick. I'm telling you; you'd like Arden if you'd just—"

"Ooh! Arden. She's so pretty and funny. I love her, Daddy. She always gives me a lollipop and tons of hugs and kisses when I visit you at work."

Little ears, AKA Vivienne, has a tendency just to appear. She's a Daddy's girl through and through, so she likes to be near him. Climbing onto my lap, she gives me a kiss on the cheek before turning to look at her father. Over her head, I give him a dirty look. The fucker didn't mention that the girl he wants to set me up with works for him.

Beaming at his little angel, Dante laughs. "Tell Uncle E how pretty Arden is, Vivi."

Fuck, I need to put a stop to this now. This kid is like a heat-seeking missile when she gets her mind on something—just like her damn father.

"No, no, no! Vivi, your daddy is just joking. Let's talk about how smart and amazing you are instead. Tell me all about how you're doing in preschool."

God bless her, she immediately starts talking about what's been happening at school. Smirking at Dante over Viv's head, I breathe out a sigh of relief that I've managed to avoid what would likely have been an absolute shit show. I've gotten to the ripe old age of thirty-five by avoiding fix-ups and blind dates, and I have no intention of changing.

chapter two

Exton

ENTERING THE CLUB, I'M met with loud music, strobe lights, and beautiful looking people. Clubbing isn't my scene, mostly because every damn time I come to one I somehow wind up in a fucking tabloid looking like a giant cockbag.

I'm here tonight because I've missed a shitload of events over the last year while I've been on and off the set for my last project. Dante's big on family and friends, and I hated to let him down. It'd be great if Laz could be here too; it helps to have a wingman. Unfortunately, with the restaurant opening in a few weeks, he's busier than a one-legged man in an ass-kicking contest, so he gets a pass.

After entering the VIP area, I head right for the bar to grab a cold one. Smiling and waving at a few of the Harts I see along the way, I'm not paying attention to anything else. At least not until the most beautiful woman I've ever seen in my life—bar fucking none—walks by me. She's not my usual type at all, dark hair when I've always preferred lighter, but she's got my attention in a way that no other woman ever has.

Never in my life have I had my jaw drop open just at the sight of a woman. I'm pretty sure I didn't have this kind of reaction the first time I had sex. But this . . . This is something else entirely. She might as well just have put a leash on me because I can't keep myself from following her. Watching the sexy sway of her hips as she glides across the room in a pair of fuck-me heels is making my mouth water. Fuck—this girl. She's something different.

When she steps up to the bar to order her drink, I take the opportunity to check her out from the side. Her body is sexy as hell—full tits, curves, legs for days and the most beautiful face I've ever seen. She places her hands on the bar, and I check for rings, letting out a relieved breath when I see nothing.

Looking around, I determine that no one is watching her, which gives me hope that she's single. I sure as hell know that if she belonged to me, I'd be making sure that no one else touched her. If she does have a boyfriend, he's a piece of shit because no one worth a damn would expect a woman to get her own drink.

I'm just stepping up to the bar next to her to introduce myself as she's handed what looks like some kind of chocolate drink. Shaking my head at her choice of drinks, I watch as she takes a sip. Jesus, her fucking lips. I want them all over me, and I want to watch while she takes my dick into her mouth.

She lets out a sound of pure pleasure—half moan, half sigh, and I feel myself losing the battle not to get hard as I let out a tortured sound. Stepping up behind her I lean in so that only she can hear what I'm going to say.

"I've never wanted a chocolate drink before, but listening to that moan made me want ninety of them."

What I don't add is that I'd be open to having them poured on me so that she can lick them off, because that would be coming on too strong. Hell, what I've already said is more than I ever have before as far as coming on to a woman goes. Her hair smells like nirvana and being this close to her means that I'm really struggling not to sport a full-on tent in my fucking pants.

When she turns around, my heartbeat picks up tenfold from a few seconds earlier. Fuck, did I say she was beautiful? Because I was wrong—she's so much fucking more than that.

Now, I just need her to look me in the eye.

As someone behind me gets a little too close, I'm forced up against her. She sets her hand on my chest and pushes me back from her. "Don't touch me," she says forcefully.

Holy fuck, she's a firecracker.

Lifting my hands so that she can see that I'm not some grabby asshole I say, "Don't be angry, Beautiful. I didn't mean to close in on you like that. I just wanted to meet you."

Fuck, I am on a real downward roll tonight because I sound like an aging pimp. I'd say something else, but I'm so tongue-tied that I fear I'll make it worse. I'm going to blame the fact that the blood in my head is taking a trip to my cock for the fact that I can't seem to form decent sentences.

My cock goes from semi-hard to *holy shit this is a real fucking problem, seek cover,* in the few seconds that it's taking for her to check me out. I reassure myself that maybe, for the first time in my life, the fact that I'm a celebrity may work in my favor. At least if she realizes who I am, she'll know I'm not some perv. As she looks me over, I study her like she's a pop quiz that I'm going to have to take.

Holy fucking Christ . . . She just licked her fucking lips. Now I'm back to thinking about her licking the tip of my dick. What the fuck? I'm going nuts over this woman, and I don't even know her!

Finally, her eyes meet mine, and an electric sensation jolts me from within when I stare into her eyes. Fuck me—I think I just felt a spark. Dante might not be crazy, after all.

Staring at the beauty before me, a euphoric sensation overtakes me as I realize that she feels it too. It's all in her eyes and they're telling me quite clearly that she's just as affected. She's going to be as into exploring this as I am.

But. Fuck. Now she looks pissed. And even though it shouldn't, that just makes my dick harder. She's fascinating—and I want everything she's got. I know she's getting the connection between the two of us, I can see it in her eyes. Why is she so angry?

I feel the jolt again when she shoves at me—roughly—and walks away. Without uttering even one word.

What.

The.

Fuck?

My impulse is to chase after her, but something is telling me that isn't going to get me anywhere. No, I need to be patient for once in my life and make a plan. Keeping a respectable distance away, I watch as she walks toward Sabrina and then the two of them head for the dance floor.

Seeing my opportunity to ask Dante who the beautiful woman is, I head his way. Of course, because I'm in a fucking hurry, I keep getting stopped along the way by people saying hello. I'm just about over to where he is when he heads to the dance floor. Rolling my eyes, I head after him. The fucker is like Pavlov's dog, really. Wherever Sabrina goes, he follows.

Making my way to the edge of the dance floor, I watch as my woman—yes, I'm aware of how that sounds and *no,* I don't give a shit—dances. There's something inside of me that's desperate to get out and claim her. I take note of the other men showing interest in her, and I struggle to keep my temper in check. I want to get in the face of any motherfucker that dares look at her and tell them to back way off. What the fuck happened to me being calm, cool, and collected? I'm failing at all of the three Cs right now.

I continue doing mental gymnastics while I try to formulate a plan. This girl isn't going to be easy, obviously, and it's glaringly obvious that it's something that makes her even more attractive to me. This woman needs to be handled in a way that I have zero experience with.

The longer that I stand and stare, the more I'm able to convince myself that maybe I just caught her off guard at the bar. Fuck it; I'm going to at least try the direct approach.

Last night was an epic crash and burn. I approached her on the dance floor, and she rebuffed me again. If it weren't for the fact that she made fuck me eyes at me before she said no thank you, I'd believe that she really had no interest. The fuck of it is that I can clearly see that she's interested. Now, I just need to do whatever it takes to get her to admit it.

Meanwhile, Dante has shined me the fuck on all day. I've texted and called more than a dozen times, and he's busy each and every time. Pacing my office like a caged animal, I make another attempt to call him. I've been calling every hour on the hour and texting every half hour for the last eight hours. It's now after dinner, and if he doesn't get his ass on the phone this time, I'm driving to his house and kicking the door in. This shit is important. I need to fucking know everything about my mystery woman.

Finally—seriously, not a minute too soon—the fucker picks up his damn phone. "Damn Ex, is there a fire? You've been calling and texting all damn day. You must really want to talk to me."

He sounds smug for some reason, but I'm not going to take his temperature. What matters right now is getting the information about my girl.

"Listen up, Fuckwad McGee, I've been calling all day because it's important. Maybe next time you'll answer the phone when I call for the eighth time in a row."

His response is a yawn. "Yeah, yeah, yeah. Keep your fuckin' tampon in. What's up?"

"Last night—"

"Nice club, right?"

"Sure, yeah, great fuckin' club. There was this—"

"Sabrina loves it there, so it was a no-brainer when it came time to choose a location."

He's making me nuts right now talking about the club like I give a fuck.

"Dude, shut the fuck up about the club. I've got something important to ask you if you'd stop yammering for five goddamn seconds."

The sound of his laughter is his response. "Well, fuck me, Ex. What's got your boxers in a bunch?"

"Last night, there was a girl—"

"No shit, Einstein. I think there were several hundred of them."

"Dude, I swear to fuck, if you interrupt me one more time I'm going to go postal. Can you just listen? This shit is important, and I need to fucking find her."

"Damn," he says with a laugh. "You're serious. I've never seen you this interested in anyone before. This is a lot of effort for you to put in just to get laid."

My response is immediate and emphatic. "I'm not fucking trying to get laid," I snap. "This girl—it isn't like that. There's something there."

Running my hand along my jaw, I close my eyes and remember what she looked like—every amazing inch. "This girl was way beyond a ten—she's more like a fifteen. Long black hair, amazing lips, perfect face and a body that had me sporting wood like a teenage asshole at Hooters. She was perfect. I have to know who she is and how I can find her."

"I don't know that I saw anyone like that—"

"You did. You fucking know her. She spent most of her time with Sabrina, and you were talking to her, too."

"Oh yeah? Well, Sherlock, it sounds like you're desperate for info. You know, I think it's time that you stop being a loser so that I can fix you up with Arden."

Pulling the phone from my ear, I make a frustrated face. "Dude, are you on cough- medicine or something? I'm asking you a serious fucking question, and you're talking about setting me up with some girl that I don't give a shit about. "

"That's interesting, considering the fact that you just described her as a fifteen. But, I guess if you're not interested, I'll just hook her up with someone else."

My mind is scrambling to make sense of what he just said. Does he mean that the girl I can't stop thinking about is Arden? "Are you saying that—"

"That Arden is the fifteen? Yeah, that's what I'm saying. How fucking dumb do you feel right now?"

So stupid that there aren't even words.

chapter three

Exton

ARDEN MADE ME WORK for it, fuck, did she ever, but eventually I've finally gotten her to come around—sort of. The plain truth is that I know that I'm not out of the woods yet. Arden requires work. When I said as much to Dante, he informed me that anything worth having was worth working for. I'm working my ass off, and I won't stop. There's no doubt in my mind that she's worth every bit of effort.

We're together, and I'm not going fucking anywhere without her by my side, but she likes to pretend that it's "strictly temporary." The stubborn woman won't admit that temporary is not fucking happening. I want everything with Arden, the whole nine yards. She's my spark, and I'm more certain of that than anything else. I'm stretching my patience to the absolute limit in order to keep myself from demanding that she move in with me, and we only just made love for the first time a few hours ago.

Being inside of Arden was like sex on steroids. At one point, I was taking her so hard that I actually wondered if I was going to fuck my back out, yet I was powerless to stop. I've never wanted or needed anyone like that, ever. Fortunately, my back is intact, and, judging by the hard-on that's rubbing up against her naked ass right now, my dick's in good working condition, too.

As I run my hand up and down her arm, I bury my face in her hair and breathe in. She smells like home. Like sex and intimacy, quiet moments and adventure, laughter and a house full of kids. Yeah—I said it. Kids. I wore a condom last night, and I'll continue wearing them until I get her to admit that we're permanent. The second that happens, I'm going to work like a motherfucker to get my woman knocked up.

Trailing my hand back down her arm, I slide it forward and touch her stomach. What will it feel like once there's life in there? The idea of her being round with child is in no way a turn off. In fact, I'd have to say that it's a pretty big fucking turn on. Nothing says that a woman is yours quite like having a family.

My dick hardens more as she shifts her sexy ass against me. Fuck—I want to let her sleep, but I want to be inside of her again so goddamn bad I can fucking taste it. I try to talk myself out of it, but my body isn't so much listening to my brain. Even as I argue with myself, my hand is busy lifting the covers and pulling them off. My mouth waters when I see her luscious naked body before me, and I know exactly how I'm going to start my morning.

It doesn't take long to get her situated onto her back, and I waste no time before spreading her legs and settling myself between them. Pressing my nose to the silky soft hair at the top of her mound, I inhale. Just like last night, her scent awakens something wild within me. It calls to something inside of me—something bossy and dominant that wants to be with her forever. Lifting my head, I stare down at the heart of her. Sexy as fuck, just like everything else about her.

I've always hated having sex with hairless girls because, to me, it's a little creepy. I'm not into a jungle, but I like a little bit of mystery and I like knowing that I'm with a woman—not a girl. Arden's lips are bare of any hair—waxed, I think, judging by the silken smooth appearance and texture. What she's got is a sexy little tuft of hair on her mound that makes me want to eat her alive.

I know that she's starting to wake up as I feel her shift restlessly below me. Starting down by her knees, I run my nose along the insides of her thighs, leaving little kisses along the way. When I hear her sigh of pleasure, I start to tickle the backs of her knees as I wait for her to open her eyes.

Realizing that she needs a little extra inspiration to wake up, I return to her center and run my tongue ever so slowly from her core to her clit.

I'm rewarded with her look of shocked arousal as her eyes fly open and she looks down at me.

"What're you doing," she questions sleepily.

Chuckling at her I answer, "Getting ready to eat."

Her shocked expression and the flush that spreads across her face and down onto her chest makes me want her more than ever.

"I need to shower—"

Shaking my head at her, I let out a laugh. "I've been down here a while and I can assure you, there's no problem. I love the way you taste, and I plan to enjoy you coming on my tongue."

Blushing furiously, she turns her head. "I'm sure you're used to women getting up and freshening themselves before you wake up."

Squeezing her thighs with my hands, I drop another open mouth kiss onto her sex. When I finish kissing her clit, I lift my head to look her in the eye.

"I didn't ever stay long enough to wake up with those women, Arden. That whole bullshit morning routine wasn't for me. I don't think there's a man alive that falls for the whole *I woke up looking like this* routine. I stopped letting people spend the night once I realized that was going to keep happening. I'll tell you a secret—I hate it—and every man I know fucking hates it, too."

"You do?"

"Yeah, beautiful. Waking up with you like this is perfect to me. You're sexy as fuck right now, and I want to bite, lick, suck, eat, finger and fuck you—just the way you are. I'd suggest you get used to it because I plan to wake you up with my mouth, my fingers or my dick more often than not."

Without giving her a chance to respond, I dive in and do what I've wanted to do since the minute I woke up. She's so responsive, rolling her hips as I work my tongue around her slick sex.

I smile against her lips as her fingers slide into my hair. If I weren't able to tell that she was enjoying this by the fact that she's getting wetter by the minute, her guiding my head with her hands would clear it up for me.

I gorge myself on the taste and texture of her now soaked pussy, my need to make her come only slightly stronger than my need to be inside of her.

"Please, Exton," she pants brokenly as I slide two of my fingers into her heat and start rubbing against her g-spot.

Lifting my head, I smile when I see the look on her face. She fucking loves what I do to her body, and I love doing it.

"You ready to come, baby?"

Her answer is a desperate sounding, high-pitched whimper.

Knowing that she's right there, I drop my head again and focus on the top of her clit with my tongue. It's her hot button, and within a minute she's coming. Normally, I get annoyed when women pull my hair as they come, but with Arden, I'm getting off on her reactions.

After I've wrung every last moment out of her orgasm, I start kissing my way up her body. I swirl kisses around her abdomen, trail my tongue between her breasts—and of course I have to stop to worship the wonder twins.

That's right, I'm a grown man that's named my girlfriend's tits. Surprise, surprise, I'm a sucker for her perfect fucking rack and her deliciously sexy nipples. Sue me.

"I can't believe how much I want you," she whispers. So quietly that if I wasn't so attuned to her, I might just have missed it.

Maneuvering myself over her, I place feather soft kisses on her lips. "I want you too, beautiful."

As I lift my head, I see an expression on her face that seems to be wonder—almost as if she can't believe what's happening.

"Is it like this every time?"

"With us? Fuck yes. You can count on it, baby."

"No," she says with a soft laugh. "I meant is this what sex is always like?"

The answer is simple, and I'm not going to sugarcoat it just because I know damn well that it's going to make her panic. She's getting the truth, and I'll deal with the fallout on the other end if she gets whacked out.

"No. This is special Arden, and we both know it. This is it, beautiful."

I can practically feel the gears in her head turning, but I'm not going to let her fear put a damper on what's happening. Leaning across the bed, I grab a condom from the side table and hand it to her.

"Put this on me," I say firmly.

Her eyes snap up to mine lightning fast. "I don't really know how. They taught us on cucumbers and bananas in sex ed during high school, but—"

I can't contain the chuckle that erupts from my throat. "Consider me your human test dummy then. We're going to talk about long-term birth control, but until then we're using condoms. You're going to want to get used to putting them on me because we're going to be spending a lot of time in bed."

I give her room to maneuver so that she can sit up. Sitting back on my haunches, I watch as she opens the foil packet. It's a struggle not to beg her to hurry when she wraps her hand around my cock just below the tip. Holding me steady, she gets the condom into place and starts rolling it down. Covering her hand with mine, I help her roll it the rest of the way.

"Was I doing it wrong?"

"No, but I'm faster and I need to be inside that tight pussy right now."

Her half gasp, half giggle is enough to make me insane. Settling her back on the bed, I spread her legs and lower myself over her. After making sure that she's ready for me, I slowly begin to slide in.

Her slick heat envelops me like the tightest silken fist I've ever encountered. I want to be inside of her without anything between us so fucking bad that I swear I'd pay any amount of money to make that happen.

We both let out sounds of pleasure as I settle in as far as I can go, and I jerk against her when she grabs my ass in her hands.

"Fuck me, please," she says with a gasp.

Shaking my head at her with a laugh, I cover her mouth with mine and kiss her senseless. All the while continuing to pump slowly in and out of the most incredible woman on this fucking planet.

She breaks the kiss to let out a moan. "Faster," she cries.

"No," I say firmly. "Last night was fast. This morning is for slow and steady. I don't want it to be over quickly—I want to fuck your perfect pussy for as long as possible. I want you to come on my dick again and again. It doesn't always have to be fast to be good, beautiful. Let me show you all the ways that you can come."

I alternate between shallow and deep thrusts as I work us toward euphoria, soaking up the intensity of her reactions as we work together to get there.

"Look at me, beautiful. You feel how good we are together?"

Opening her eyes, she looks at me with eyes that are full of lust. "I do," she pants.

"It's you and me, baby. All. The. Way."

I punctuate each word with a deep thrust. My reward is the tight clench of her against my cock and the soft look in her eyes.

"Yes! Exton!"

"That's right, beautiful. Say my name while you come."

With a small adjustment of my position above her, I'm now rubbing continuously against her clit as I thrust. Seeing her like this, feeling her tight sex fluttering against my cock is amazing. Knowing that I'm doing this to her is going to take me over the edge, which could be a problem. It takes everything I have to hold on so that I don't come before her.

Arching her back, she opens her mouth in a silent scream as her orgasm hits. With a groan of relief, I let myself go. "Fuck, Arden!"

I stay inside of her for as long as I can, but the fact that I'm wearing a condom means that time is of the essence. I need to get myself out of her and dispose of the damn thing. With a sigh, I drop a kiss on her lips before pulling out.

After getting rid of the condom and using the bathroom, I come back into the bedroom to find her asleep. Laughing quietly, I shake my head. Apparently great lovemaking puts my woman out.

Realizing that this means I need something else to encourage her to wake up, I head to the kitchen to make her a coffee. After stirring in the insane amount of sweetener that she likes, I stroll back into the bedroom to wake her up so that we can shower together.

Now that we've showered, I'm waiting for Arden to finish drying her hair. The plan is to go to the movies. You could've knocked me over with a feather when she chose an action flick instead of the new rom-com that everyone is currently raving about.

This is the first time I've ever spent in her apartment where I've got the opportunity to take it all in. I walk around and check out the two personal photos—one with her and a woman I'm assuming is a family member because they look a lot alike, and one of her as a child with two older looking people on a beach. That's pretty much the sum total of the personalization in the room.

Looking around, it dawns on me that I've not seen any sign of reading material. I always assumed that if I were to fall for a woman, she'd be as avid a reader as I am. Judging by the complete lack of any books, it doesn't seem like Arden reads very much, if at all. I'm really surprised, to be honest. If I'd had to guess, I would've said that she spent a lot of time reading.

"Looking for clues about me, Mr. Alexander?"

I laugh as I turn to look at her as she walks into the living room.

"I was just looking around and I noticed that you don't have even one book in here. You don't enjoy reading?"

Instead of laughing, she tenses up and crosses her arms over her chest. Looking away from me, she shakes her head. "No, I don't. Books aren't my thing."

Certain that I've somehow stepped into one of her no-go areas, I say nothing else. Still, I tuck it away in my head to think about later. There's something about the subject of books that upsets her—now I just need to figure out what it is.

chapter four

Exton

THEY SAY THAT RELATIONSHIPS change people, and they're right. I hate the fucking phone. Yet, since I started dating Arden, I'm never without my cell phone. Right now, I'm at the restaurant going over business stuff with Laz, and I've checked it no fewer than five times in the last half hour.

"Hey, asshole, what's up with you and the phone? Waiting for the results of your moron test?"

Rolling my eyes, I choke out a laugh. "You know damn well that I'm checking to see if Arden has texted. Don't make fun of me, you dick."

With a wave of his hand, Laz laughs my insult off. "I never thought I'd see the day, man. Not only are you ass over elbows in love, but you're checking your damn phone more than once a day. It's a fucking miracle."

"It sure as hell feels like it," I answer. "Being with her has changed everything. All that shit Dante has talked about the spark? It kills me to admit it, but the fucker was right. Arden isn't just a spark—she's a permanent firework."

"You realize you sound like a bitch, right?"

"No, what I sound like is a man in love, and there's nothing wrong with that. You should try it sometime."

"Oh, fuck me—are you going all Dante on me? I don't think I can deal with two of you in love mode."

I'm laughing as I flip him the bird. "Shut it, fuckhead."

"I'm just fucking with you," he laughs. "I think it's great that you've finally found someone. The fact that you took the big step and issued a press release making it clear that she's your woman was a huge move for you. I like seeing you so happy."

"I like it too," I answer honestly. "I like it a lot."

It's Friday night, and I've been waiting for hours for Arden to get off work and get herself over here. I had offered to pick her up and chauffer her over, but she wasn't having it. I'm not stupid; I know she needs the reassurance of knowing that she could leave anytime she wants to. I don't see that happening, and I don't think she does either, but if that's the security she needs, so be it.

Gripping Arden's hand in mine, I lead her into my house. It took some time to get her to agree to start spending time here, but I've finally done it. I'm pretty certain that every day I get past more of the emotional wall she had built around herself.

Looking around the entryway, she smiles and lets out what sounds like a relieved breath. "I was worried that it would be—"

Slapping her hand over her mouth, she giggles. "Never mind."

I fucking love when my woman laughs—but I hate when she tries to keep things to herself. Wrapping my arms around her, I drop a kiss onto her lips.

"Beautiful, you know I'm not going to write that off. Tell me what you were worried about."

Worrying at her lower lip with her teeth, she sighs. "I was worried that it might be—not homey. If that even makes any sense."

"It does, but you should've realized that my house is a Hart design, it could never be tacky."

"Ohhhh," she drawls. "I didn't realize you had Dante build the house. I guess I should've clued into that as soon as the door opened. It's a beautiful home."

"I like it," I say simply.

I take her from room to room and show her through the house, smiling as she shows interest in things along the way. Showing her the theater room, I inform her that we'll be watching The Walking Dead there every Sunday night. I can tell that I've made her happy because her answering smile lights up her entire face.

Coming to the last room on the tour, I guide her inside my bedroom. Looking around, she nods her head.

"This suits you," she says. "It's classic—timeless. Nothing is loud or . . . fluffy."

Hmm. Maybe she doesn't love it as much as she could. I'm willing to make some changes if need be.

"Do you think that I should add some fluff? Anything you need to make you feel comfortable here—"

Placing her hand over my mouth, she shakes her head. "It's perfect—I wouldn't change anything."

She's not one hundred percent comfortable, but she's close enough that I believe it won't take forever to get her to feel at home. Arden has come a long way in a short period, and I'm not going to pretend that I don't take pride in that. My woman is a warrior—and I'm lucky as hell that I got her to put down her weapons long enough to let me in.

"I know this is a big step for you, and to make you feel more at home I've got something special coming for you. We should go hang out in the living room until it comes."

"Ooh," she squeaks out excitedly. "What is it? Tell me!"

"Nope—but trust me, you're going to love it. Come on."

Squeezing her hand in mine, I lead her back downstairs to the den. I sit down on the couch before pulling her down onto my lap for a kiss.

I like this—my woman in my home. She fits. We fit. I think she knows it but just hasn't gotten to the point where she can say it out loud and own it just yet. The funny thing is that I always assumed that if it ever came down to it, I would be the one dragging my feet about getting serious and committing to someone. That hasn't happened at all. I don't know how to explain it other than to say that the certainty I have that she's it—that we're forever—is rock solid.

Ending the kiss, I trace my thumb over her lips. "How was work?"

Setting her head against my shoulder, she smiles. "It was good—the usual, really. I can't complain. I like working at Hart."

"So your boss isn't a total dick," I question with a laugh.

"Not at all. When I came out of college, I had no idea what to do with myself. I was so lost and after everything that had happened . . . Well—getting in at Hart was a godsend. In addition to being a great job, I got a great friend in Sabrina. I couldn't ask for more."

"What happened in college, beautiful?"

She says nothing in response and enough time passes that I assume she's not going to.

"Not yet," she says quietly. "I'm getting there, and I want to tell you, I'm just not ready yet. Soon."

Kissing the top of her head, I nod. "Soon," I agree.

We're sitting in silence for no more than a few moments when the doorbell rings. Realizing that the surprise is here, I help Arden to her feet. Linking my hand with hers, I guide her to the front door.

"What is it?" she giggles.

Opening the door, I drink in her squeal of surprise with a smile.

"No way," she exclaims from behind me as I take the delivery bags from her favorite Chinese place.

After thanking the driver, I close the door and head right for the kitchen.

"You've got to be about six miles outside of the delivery area," she muses. "How did you get them to deliver all the way out here?"

Grabbing plates and cutlery, I set everything out on the table. "Mrs. Tan is a softy," I answer. "I went in offering her the world, but she wanted to do it for free. In the end, we compromised. She and Mr. Tan now have gift certificates for ten dinners at Laz's. We worked it out that I'll order early on Fridays so that they don't lose a driver during peak time, and it works out for everyone. In addition to having the best Chinese restaurant in LA, the Tans are also awesome people."

As I'm explaining, Arden is opening a container of eggrolls. Taking a bite of one, she nods as I finish talking. "It's pretty lame how excited I am that I get to keep on enjoying the Tans' food on Fridays. I think I'm falling in love with yo—erm, I mean, I love that you did this."

I let her off the hook without comment, because that was a confirmation that I'm right about what she's feeling. We're on the right path here.

chapter five

Exton

"ARDEN, DO YOU THINK that when I grow up I can be a cowgirl?"

I love seeing Arden interact with my niece and nephews because, to me, it's a preview of things to come. The fact that they loved her before I even knew her doesn't hurt at all. It's nice to see her let her softest side out.

"Of course, Vivi. You can be anything that you want."

Clapping excitedly, Vivi beams. "Daddy took me to the bookstore this morning and got me another Nellie Sue book! She's the bestest cowgirl in the whole world."

"Ah, the bookstore," Arden says longingly. "When I was your age, it was my very favorite place to go. I thought books were magical."

I can't take my eyes off of her. The look on her face is off, and something about it is making me feel uncomfortable.

"Mommy says that books are magic too," Vivi squeals happily. "I used to want to be a Princess like Aurora from Sleeping Beauty. Did you want to be a Princess when you were little?"

Her hesitation and the expression on her face are heartbreaking.

"I guess I did," she finally answers.

"Did you want to marry a Prince and wear a big white dress?"

The pained look that flashes across Arden's face stops me dead. There's a story there, and I don't know what the hell it is, but I need to find out.

"Sure," Arden says in a voice that is almost totally devoid of any enthusiasm.

"I wanted that too," Vivi says excitedly. "But then I started reading about Nellie Sue and now I don't want to wear big dresses no more."

Twirling a piece of Vivi's hair between two fingers, Arden laughs. "I bet those big dresses could be a pain."

"Have you ever read any cowgirl books, Arden?"

"I haven't," Arden says.

"Well, my Aunt Minnie has a big room in her house with lots and lots of books and I love to sit in there and read with her. Maybe you could come over with me, and we can look for a big girl cowgirl book. If we find one, you could take it to your house! Do you have a big room with books there?"

Shaking her head, Arden looks off into the distance. "I don't," she says. "When I grew up I didn't have time to read anymore."

Gasping dramatically, Vivi bounces on Arden's lap. "You have time now," she exclaims. "My new book is right inside. Will you read my Nellie Sue book to me?"

"Of course, sweetie. I'd be happy to read your story to you."

Not wanting Arden to realize that I was so closely monitoring that discussion, I turn to Sabrina and Dante and feign interest in their conversation. I don't know what, but there is something going on with Arden and books.

Vivi is back in a matter of seconds. Climbing back onto Arden's lap, she hands her the book and patiently waits for her to start reading.

My heart melts as I watch Arden read to Vivi. Noticing that I don't hear Dante and Sabrina talking anymore, I turn my head and find that they're both taking it in as well. Vivi giggles as Arden continues reading, and my attention goes right back to them.

She's so engaging that I'm not even surprised to see that my nephews, Jack and Cooper, have taken interest in the story. Slowly but surely, they've made their way over to her, and now Jack is on one side of her chair and Cooper the other. She's good with kids—amazing, even.

As she finishes, Vivi claps her hands and giggles happily. "More! More!"

"That's the end, silly," Arden laughs.

"Aunt Minnie says the story doesn't have to be over if you use your 'magination! Can you do that? That's my favorite!"

A look of longing flashes across Arden's face so quickly that I don't have time to figure out what it is in response to.

"I'll try," she tells Vivi with a nervous laugh. "I'm not sure how good I'll be at it."

Taking a deep breath, she carries on with Nellie Sue's story. My jaw hangs open as she takes the reigns of the story with no pause, and I get wrapped up listening to her. She's got an amazing talent for putting a story together, and I'm now confused as to why she didn't get a job in the arts. It's clear to me now that she's incredibly gifted.

By the time she's finished, all three of the kids are beaming happily at her, completely enraptured by the tale that she wove.

"Wow, Arden," Jack says. "You should write books. I don't normally like listening to Vivi's story time, but you made it so good that I didn't even care that it was a girl story."

Everyone laughs at that—except for Arden. Sure, she smiles, but the expression doesn't reach her eyes. She looks fragile, and I don't like it at all. Standing from my chair, I walk over to her. Lifting Vivi up, I give her a quick kiss and tell her to go tickle her father.

As soon as Vivi heads off to do just that, I take Arden's hand and pull her toward me. Wrapping an arm around her, I bring her to me so that I can get her mind off whatever just upset her. "I think we should head home," I say huskily. "Maybe work off some of this dinner. What do you think?"

Ducking her head against my chest, she lets out a chuckle. "I think that sounds like a great idea."

Arriving back at my house, I stop in the bathroom to grab a condom and then take Arden into the back yard. After turning the hot tub jets on, I peel off my shirt. Wiggling my eyebrows at her I say, "Time to get naked, baby."

"Exton! I'm not—I can't do that. It's too embarrassing." Her face is red even imagining it, so I know she's being honest.

Disregarding her words, I take off my shoes, socks, jeans and briefs. Standing before her, completely naked and obviously aroused, I take her hand in mine and bring it to my dick. The fact that her hand immediately fists my cock tells me that it isn't my nakedness that's the issue.

"Does it embarrass you that I'm naked right now?"

Licking her lips, she shakes her head. "No—but it's not your naked body that would embarrass me, it's mine. I can't be out here naked—it's bad enough that I do it in the bedroom."

"That's bullshit," I answer firmly. "You've got to stop this shit, beautiful. You're my fucking woman, and if it's an option to have your sexy ass naked, I'm taking it. Here, the car, the bedroom or anywhere else—I don't care. You're as beautiful out here as you are everywhere else. Stop telling yourself otherwise because it's nothing but bullshit."

Worrying at her lower lip with her teeth, she stares at me as she processes what I just said. "I don't know—"

"You don't, but *I do*. Does this feel like the dick of a guy who doesn't want to think you're the sexiest woman alive?"

"But you were used to perfection," she argues.

"No," I answer truthfully. "I never had perfection until now, baby. Anything that came before you can't compare."

"I don't know how you can say that—"

"I can say it because it's true. I wish that you understood how I felt. I get that you don't, yet, but when you do, you'll feel so silly for ever thinking that you're anything less than the most amazing woman in the world to me."

She's always beautiful, but the light flush on her cheeks as she smiles shyly at me makes her even more so.

"I think you're quite something too," she says softly.

She accentuates her words with a twist of her wrist as she runs her hand very slowly up and down my shaft. I'd love nothing more than to help her to her knees so that she can suck my cock, but right now it's more important to get her out of her clothes. Grasping her hand in mine, I stop her from shuttling up and down.

"You won't make me forget why we're out here you know," I say with a laugh. "Time to get naked, baby. Strip down so that I can get my hands and tongue all over you."

Sighing with clear exasperation, she shakes her head. "You're not going to let this go, are you?"

"Nope. Get naked."

"Ugh. Fine."

Stepping back from me, she makes quick work of getting her tee shirt off, immediately followed by her bra. I'm helpless to contain my growl of appreciation when I see her hot fucking rack on full display. The fucking wonder twins have an exclusive and extremely devoted fan club—me.

My dick twitches so hard that I have no choice but to fist it and give it a tug. "Unbelievable that you don't realize how fucking hot you are, baby."

My words cause her to stand up a bit straighter, and I know that my honesty helps her get ahold of her nerves. After kicking off her sandals, she opens the button and zipper on her shorts. Pulling them down, she takes them off and sets them on the chair she's already got her shirt and bra on. Standing before me in only a pair of sexy hot pink panties, she's a fucking sight.

"The underwear," I growl.

After skimming them down over her hips and setting them on the chair with the rest of her clothes, she immediately launches herself into my arms. Circling my arms around her, I cup her ass in my hands and pull her to me before covering her lips with mine.

Kissing this woman has quickly become one of my favorite things in the world. I love the way she tastes, the feeling of her perfect lips beneath mine and fuck me if she doesn't know how to work her tongue. As we're kissing, I somehow manage to keep enough of my wits about me to maneuver us toward the hot tub—without causing us to fall in.

Pulling my lips from hers, I smile down at her as her eyes open and she stares at me with what I've come to think of as the look. It's part arousal, part need, and part surprise—like she can't believe that we're this good together. I think there's still a part of her that thinks this is all going to blow up—but I also think that every day that goes by takes away a little more of her fear.

"See," I say huskily. "Being naked outside isn't bad."

Laughing softly, she leans in and kisses my chest. "Your powers of persuasion are quite something. You could probably talk me into walking naked down Hollywood Boulevard during rush hour."

I let out a chuckle as I turn her so that I can walk us into the hot tub.

"Don't worry, beautiful. That will never happen—I only want you naked for me. You know the rules—no one else gets this."

Tapping the slate on the side of the hot tub I say, "Sit that sexy ass down right here."

She complies even as she lifts her brow in silent question.

"You know I like to eat first," I growl.

Gliding my hands up her thighs, I spread them gently so that she's positioned where I want her. Taking in the sight before me, I grin when I see that she's already wet for me.

"Mm," I rasp "Looks like someone's ready to be my main course."

After positioning myself so that I'm able to put her legs over my shoulders, I lean in and drop several quick kisses on her mound and the soaked lips of her sex. Grabbing her ass with my hands, I hold her where I want her as I begin running my tongue over her swollen lips.

Over and over I trace my tongue all around as I wait for her to make the sound that tells me she's desperate. The sound of her groan from above me is music to my ears. I smile as I let go of her sexy ass and maneuver her legs wider. Spreading her lips with my thumbs, I start working my tongue against her clit. Fisting my hair in her hands, she bucks against my mouth.

"Oh, oh!"

Thrusting two fingers into her tight cunt, I thrust them in and out as I pick up the pace with my tongue.

"Ah! Exton . . . fuck! Exton!"

I can feel her arousal coating my lips, my tongue, and my chin as I work her harder, and all that's doing is making me want to fuck her until she screams. Loudly. I'm barely hanging on to my last shred of self-control as she comes with a loud cry.

Pulling my fingers from her, I grab the condom I left on the side. Standing, I tear open the foil packet.

"Stop," she says huskily. "We aren't going to be needing the condom."

Whipping my head up in confusion, I find her staring at me with a smile.

"I'm ready," she says firmly. "My birth control is in effect and I'm ready for it to be just us. We don't need to use condoms anymore."

We've talked about this, and I knew she had gone on birth control, but I haven't wanted to pressure her to take this step before she was ready. I made the choice hers—and knowing that she's ready to be skin on skin with me is mind blowing. Its's not just that I'll be inside of her bare. It's the knowledge that she's opening herself up more to me. This isn't a decision she would make if her heart weren't involved.

I toss the condom onto the hot tub deck with shaking hands. I'm going to be inside of her, bare. I've never gone bare—not even once. Not only am I ready to take that step with her; I'm also about to go pure caveman and fill her with come over and over again.

I'd planned to take her inside the hot tub, but knowing that I'm about to be inside of her with no barrier, I've changed my mind. Climbing out of the water, I sit down on the slate deck, leaving my legs dangling in the water.

"Straddle me," I say simply.

"I thought—"

"The first time I feel you with nothing, I want it just to be us. I want to feel you—not the water, not anything else. Just you."

Helping her get situated on top of me, I let out a tortured moan as I feel her small hand grab my dick. Holding me firmly, she guides me to her drenched opening. We both let out sounds of pleasure as she rubs the tip of me against her pussy. Gritting my teeth, I force myself to start thinking about long division. I need the distraction to center myself because one touch of her heat on my bare cock has me damn near ready to blow.

I completely lose my train of thought as she begins to sink down on me and her slick walls surround me. Fuck, maybe going skin to skin wasn't a great idea. I'm seconds away from an early finish.

Realization that I need to take control, now, hits me. Gripping her ass, I pull her down onto my lap, filling her the rest of the way. Throwing her head back, she cries out my name as she shudders above me. My dick pulses inside of her as I let out a tortured sound of my own.

"Grab my shoulders and hold on," I instruct. "This is going to be hard and fast."

The second she complies I start working her up and down on my shaft. The pressure of her tight cunt in combination with the heat of her arousal dripping down my cock is too fucking much.

"You feel fucking amazing, beautiful. Such a tight, wet little cunt, and you're so fucking hot. I can feel how much you like riding this dick."

The gasp she lets out corresponds with the feeling of her spasming on my shaft.

"That's right, baby. Feel how good we are skin to skin?"

"Yes," she cries. "Yes!"

I'm lifting her up and down fast and hard now, and I can feel my balls tightening up. "Work that dick, baby. Your pussy is about to be so full of my come—"

Throwing her head back, she lets out a yell as she starts to come. The feeling of her losing control sends me over the edge. I lose my ability to breathe as I start to come harder than I ever have.

"Fuck! Arden!"

I lose everything but the feeling of my dick jerking inside of her over and over as my cock erupts. When I'm finally able to take a breath, I gasp for air like a fish out of water. Intense doesn't even begin to describe what just happened. Wrapping my arms around her, I hug her to me as tightly as possible.

It takes a minute or two to be able to breathe normally again. I take that time to enjoy the after effects of the most intense lovemaking I've ever experienced. I thought we'd reached the highest high before, but now I know that we've just scratched the surface.

I'll need a lifetime to discover all of the ways to be with this woman—and I damn well intend to make sure that happens.

chapter six

Exton

WALKING INTO DANTE AND Sabrina's, I'm greeted by my niece and nephews yelling my name and running toward me to give me hugs. Not a bad way to be greeted, and I can't help but imagine how it'll be to have children of my own to go home to.

"It's Friday, Uncle E. It's a Mom day and that means Dad's at work," Cooper informs me after they've all finished saying hello.

Gesturing toward their mom I say, "I didn't come to see Dad, Bud. I came to pick your mother's brain."

"Ooh," Vivi squeals. "Like we've got another mission? Do you need my help, Uncle E?"

Giving me a pointed look, Sabrina picks Vivi up and tickles her. "No more missions, little girl. Let's take Uncle E into the kitchen with us so that you can keep working with your Playdough and he and I can talk."

Trailing after them, I take a seat at the kitchen island. After settling the kids where their Playdough is set up, Rina takes a seat next to me.

"What's up?"

I'm not here to beat around the bush, so I'm just going to be direct. "Last weekend when Arden was reading to Vivi, you saw that got weird, right?"

"Couldn't have missed it," she confirms.

"Be straight with me here, Rina—do you have any idea what that was all about?"

She shakes her head as she replies. "No. It's not the first time I've seen her freeze up about reading though, which is . . . odd."

Raking my hand through my hair, I let out a frustrated breath. "Things are great with us, so believe me, I'm not complaining. The thing is; I know that she's holding onto something. We've talked about it, and she's assured me that she'll tell me when she's ready—I just want that to be now. I hate that she feels like she needs to hide anything from me at all."

"Don't take it personally—"

"Do you know what happened to her that made her close off for so long?"

"No, I don't. She's only just recently opened up that there's anything to know. There's something in her past that she blames herself for. I know that she's ashamed of whatever went on, but I don't know what it is."

I'm silent for a few seconds as I think about Rina's words. I hate that my woman feels shame about anything. Arden is amazing—the most intriguing person I've ever known. I wish that she understood that about herself.

"How do I get her to open up to me? I mean—how did you finally break Dante down? I know that had to have been a job and a half."

Laughing softly, she shakes her head. "I just loved him. No more, no less. Where Arden's concerned, I think that you're already making a huge difference. She's letting her guard down, and she's happier than I've ever seen her. I'm not saying she was a miserable person before, but she was scared and hiding from life. With you, she's coming out of her shell. Just keep doing what you're doing. When she's ready, she'll open up."

Falling in love has actually been pretty damn good for my productivity. I used to write late into the night but since Arden came into my life, my entire schedule has changed. Now, I get up when she leaves for the day, and I generally write the entire time she's at work. It turns out that having a more normal schedule is exactly what I needed. I'm not just getting work done—I'm actually ahead of my deadlines.

Sitting in my home office working on my script, I'm starting to think about wrapping it up for the day as the phone rings. Assuming that it's Arden letting me know she's coming home, I pick up my cell without checking the caller ID.

"You on your way, beautiful?"

"Ex, we need to talk."

It's not Arden—it's Laz—and he doesn't sound happy.

"What's up?"

"Where's your fucking house phone?"

Looking over at where the phone should be, I see that the base is empty. Shrugging my shoulders, I answer, "Who the fuck knows. I'm thinking about turning it off entirely, really. Who uses that thing anyway?"

"Your fucking manager is who," he snaps. "He's been trying to call you for the last twenty minutes. As usual, when he couldn't reach you, he called me. We need to talk."

My palms immediately get clammy, and my stomach starts to churn. Lightning doesn't strike twice, I assure myself. I'm with Arden now—there are no more sex tapes. Before her, I was a fucking lunatic about making sure that I only ever had sex in places that I chose. Generally, that meant the house I kept specifically for such things or a hotel room that I would choose at random.

"Please don't fucking tell me there's another sex tape. I don't think I could handle that shit, and I can't even imagine what that would do to—"

"It's not you," he interrupts. "It's about Arden."

Now my heart is pounding triple time. "What about her?" I snap.

"I fucking hate being the one to tell you this—but about half an hour ago two nude photos from someone claiming to be her ex-husband were released. He's saying he's got more and that they'll go to the highest bidder."

No. This can't be right. Arden was never married. She'd have told me if she had been. The pictures can't be real.

"My woman's never been married before," I say firmly.

"Don't shoot the messenger," he says calmly. "Apparently she was—to some fuckstick named Ricky Greenway. Details are sketchy right now because the story is just breaking, but I told your manager to get fucking on that and find out everything he can."

I stand up so fast that my chair topples over behind me. "No one is buying pictures of my fucking woman," I snap. "We need to get on this and nip it in the bud before anyone finds out."

"I'm sorry Ex, but it's too late for that. Your manager says that gossip sites are already bidding on the rest of the photos—"

"No, goddammit, you find me a way to get in touch with whoever the fuck this Ricky Greenway is and you find it now! I can't have naked pictures of my girlfriend on the Internet, goddammit! How many pictures were there, and what was the sale price? I'll double it—fuck, I'll quadruple it!"

"Listen to me! You know from experience that isn't going to work," Laz says firmly. "It's too late to change what's happening. We need to get on damage control—"

"No! I refuse to believe that it's too late to get them back! You're not understanding what the fuck I'm saying right now—I cannot fucking deal with this shit!"

I'm so sick to my stomach that I want to hurl. I barely survived my sex tape—I can't handle Arden being put through this. I know her—and I know that if this shit happens, she'll run. I can't fucking let that happen. I need to save her from this.

"Fuck it," I snap, "You call my manager and tell him to get the contact information. I'm calling my attorney. Arden should be home any—"

I stop short when I hear the squeal of tires on my driveway. Praying that she just got home, I run to the front door and fling it open—just in time to see her taillights passing through my gate.

She must've heard me talking to Laz about the pictures, and now she's doing exactly what I feared she would do—run away.

"FUCK!"

chapter seven

Arden

THE GPS DIRECTS ME to a beautiful house in Brentwood. When I called Sabrina and told her that I needed a place to go where no one would look, she immediately told me that I could use her parents' old house. She and her sister have kept it all of these years in the hopes that some day one of their children will want to use the house. For now, they use it as guest quarters for business guests a few times a year. I let out a relieved breath when I see that Sabrina's car is already in the driveway. After parking beside her, I head for the front door.

She opens it before I have the chance to knock. Without hesitation, I fall into her arms as I sob. Guiding me inside, she closes the door behind us and lets me cry on her shoulder.

"I'm s-s-so s-s-stupid," I wail.

"Arden, no! That's not true at all. You're smart, brave and beautiful. No one deserves to have anything like this happen to them. I hate that you've held all of this in for so long."

"I w-w-was ashamed," I sob.

"You aren't the one that should be ashamed, honey. The little bit you told me on the phone was enough for me to know that. Don't let this asshole push you down again. I know you're upset and embarrassed—that's natural. But I also know that you're a fighter. Even if you don't realize that about yourself, the people that know you do. That includes Exton. He's beside himself right now because you won't answer your phone."

That makes me cry harder. The worst thing is that I've known for a while that I have been falling for him. Tonight when I heard him on the phone and my heart broke, I realized that I'm not falling anymore. I'm officially there—totally in love with him.

"He was so mad, Rina. You didn't h-h-hear him! He said . . . he said he couldn't d-d-deal with this!"

Guiding me to the couch, Sabrina sits me down, handing me a tissue before dropping down next to me.

"I'm one-hundred percent certain that you took that the wrong way," she says calmly. "Exton worships you, Arden. He would never turn his back on you. Ever."

"N-n-no, but he doesn't want to have to be involved. He's probably ashamed—"

"Why would he be ashamed?"

"Because he doesn't want or need this kind of publicity. I know he cares, but I also know what I heard. I s-s-saved him the hassle of having to tell me it's o-o-over by leaving."

Setting a hand on my shoulder, Sabrina gives a comforting squeeze. "He's called Dante and me no fewer than forty times since you left his house. He's beside himself with worry, and all he cares about is being with you. If he wanted to break up with you, he wouldn't be doing any of this. He's not letting you go, Arden. You need to calm yourself down and call him."

Wiping at my tears with the tissue, I shake my head emphatically. "He's just being nice. He can't really want to deal with this."

"I'm not being nice, beautiful, and I sure as shit am not fucking going anywhere. Come what may, you and I are in this together."

Lifting my head in shock, I find Exton walking into the living room with Dante right behind him. Without another word, Exton barrels toward me. Dropping onto the couch, he pulls me onto his lap and wraps his arms around me.

"We're never going to be over, Arden. What you heard me saying to Laz, you took the wrong way. When I said that I couldn't deal with it—what I meant was that I couldn't deal with watching you crumble. I've been there, baby. I know how fucking awful it feels and how wretched the violation is. I wouldn't wish this on my worst enemy, much less the woman I worship."

I cry harder, completely overwhelmed by his words. When I can speak, I tell him the truth. "I'm scared. I don't want people seeing me like that—"

"I know, baby . . ." He stops as his voice cracks. "I'm so fucking sorry. If I weren't famous this wouldn't have happened—"

Shaking my head emphatically, I cover his mouth. "No, Exton. This isn't your fault—it's mine. I'm the idiot that married that piece of garbage. I was nothing more than a means to an end. He ruined me just to win a bet."

Pulling back from me, Exton looks at me in shock. "He did what?"

Clasping his hand in mine, I take a deep breath. "It's time that I tell you what happened."

Dante and Sabrina stand at the same time. Looking at me, Sabrina says, "We'll go—"

Rubbing my eyes with my free hand, I shake my head. "I'd really like you to stay. I try so hard not to think about this that it's going to be hard to get the words out. I want you to know what happened, but I don't think that I can say it more than once."

With a nod of understanding, she takes Dante's hand, and they sit back down. Once they're in place, I turn my attention back to Exton. For the first time in years—since the day that I had to detail for my attorney every wretched moment—I tell the complete story of what happened back in Small Towne.

Exton never lets me go, nor does he take his eyes off of me. I know that my story is hard for him to hear, and I can clearly see how upset he is. The fact that he holds his anger in so that he can support me means everything.

Looking down the couch, I see that Dante is holding Sabrina as she cries. When I look at her, she wipes at her eyes with a tissue.

"I'm not a violent person," she says. "But if I ran into this asshole in a dark alley, I would be very tempted to run him over. I am so sorry that you went through that, Arden. It isn't fair. I hate that you gave up your writing dreams because of them. I hate that their games made you believe that true love doesn't exist. Don't let them take anything else away from you," she says emphatically.

"No, it isn't fair," I answer honestly. "But, believe it or not," I say softly, "I feel a little better now that I've gotten it off my chest. The worst thing for me has always been the idea of people that I care about knowing what happened to me because it's embarrassing. But now that I've told you—it's like a weight is off. I'm going to deal with this, and when it's over, I'm not going to let them have any more of me. Now that you all know, it's like . . . I don't know how to explain it, really. It just helps."

It really does. I never realized what a difference it would make to shine a light on it, as opposed to keeping it in the dark.

chapter eight

Arden

AFTER TALKING TO DANTE and Sabrina, Exton and I decide to stay here at her parents' old house. The only way for us to deal with what's happening right now is to stay out of the public eye. Obviously the reporters know where Exton lives, and clearly they found my house, so we're going off the grid for now.

They've gone to pick us up dinner since we can't leave the house or take the chance that a delivery person would recognize either of us, which means that Exton and I are alone. I'm anxious to look at the pictures that are online. It just has to be done. The bottom line is that I can't avoid it forever, so I'm not going to try. Exton has already tried to argue with me about it—I love him even more for trying to protect me—but I need to stop running.

"I'm going to look first," he says firmly. "Let me see how bad it is so that I can prepare you."

I'm not going to argue with that. Obviously I was dead asleep when the photos were taken, and I have no idea just how bad it's going to be. Knowing Ricky and his friends and how awful they were, I have no doubt it's going to be awful.

Pulling out his cell phone, he does a search to find the pictures. It takes just a few seconds for it to come up—something that I can see upsets him. Obviously the photos are everywhere.

Swallowing past the bile that's rising in my throat, I take a deep breath and try to calm myself down. I silently remind myself over and over that this too shall pass. It has to. My eyes are glued to Exton as he looks at the pictures. When a smile spreads across his face, and he lets out a whoop, my head rears back in shock.

Turning to me he drops a kiss on my lips. "Baby, it isn't you!"

My jaw hits the ground fast. "What?"

Bringing the phone up for me to see, he shows me the picture. Immediately my stomach starts to shoot back up my throat, because it is me—I don't know how he doesn't see that. I'm positioned on my hands and knees on top of rumpled black sheets. My mind trips over that for a second because there weren't black sheets at the Motel 6, but I'm so overwhelmed that I can't focus on that thought.

In the photo, my face is down but you can see my long black hair and the corner of my forehead. Looking down, I see that my legs are spread, and there's a vibrator sticking out of my ass—

I'm mid freak-out when I see what it is that Exton saw. On the lower left thigh of the girl in the photo, there's a black mole. And now that I'm really looking, I can't help but notice that this girl has tan lines. My skin, from head to toe, is pale and completely unblemished. I can't tan—ever. I never really get any color, no matter how hard I try.

The second photo is basically the same; only the girl is turned over onto her back. This one still only shows the bottom of the black hair—no face shots, which isn't a surprise now that I realize that this is all bullshit. In this photo, the girl has her fingers spreading the lips of her vagina. Not only is she hairless—something I've never been—but she's also got acrylics.

I'm allergic to fake nails. I had them put on one time in junior high in an attempt to fit in. The swelling around my fingers and the itching were so bad that the manicurist didn't even get to finish one hand. I'd missed a day of school because I was so looped on Benadryl. The funny thing is that Exton knows that about me—but the asshole I married clearly doesn't.

"I'm going to fucking destroy this motherfucker," Exton says darkly. "We're going to sue them until they have nothing left to be sued for."

This is where I, as the peaceful girlfriend, would normally encourage my man to calm down. I'm not doing that. Ricky Greenway and his gang of fuckwits deserve everything that is about to happen to them.

Throwing myself into his arms, I kiss him hard. The intense feeling of relief that is coursing through me has me feeling almost giddy. "It's not me," I cry happily.

"Never thought I'd be so glad to see pictures of a naked woman that is most definitely not you," he answers.

That makes me laugh, which in turn makes him laugh. We're both cracking up when there's a cough from the doorway. Looking toward the kitchen, I see Dante and Sabrina have come back. Currently, they're staring at Exton and me like we've lost all of our marbles.

"The pictures—" I begin.

"Aren't of my fucking woman," Exton exclaims triumphantly.

Sabrina heads for me like a missile, bending down and enveloping me in a hug. As the two of us talk, I feel Exton get up from the couch. After Sabrina takes his seat, the two of us keep on talking about how much of a relief it is that it's not me in the photos.

Meanwhile, I can see that Dante and Exton are standing in the kitchen, and I know that they're plotting. At this point all I can hope is that this will be resolved quickly—I don't want to live my life hiding in someone else's house. Now, more than ever, I don't want to hide anymore at all.

It's well after midnight by the time Exton and I are heading to bed. Lawyers have been called, a press release has been made, and anything that could be done has been done. Now, we just need to deal with the fallout.

As I'm walking into the bathroom to get ready for bed, it dawns on me that I don't have any clothes with me. Neither does Exton, now that I think of it. Walking back into the bedroom, I find him sitting on the bed fiddling with the TV remote.

"We don't have any clothes," I say tiredly.

"That's great news," he says with a laugh. "My plan to get you into a clothing-free environment has finally come to fruition."

Leaning against the doorway to the bathroom, I shake my head at him. "We can't walk around naked—"

"The fuck we can't," he chuckles. "Don't worry about it, beautiful. We sleep naked every night to begin with, so this is no different."

Letting out a laugh, I shrug my shoulders. "You're such a man," I say simply.

Turning back into the bathroom, I start exploring the large basket of bath products on the counter. After choosing shampoo, conditioner, and body wash, I head into the shower and turn all the jets on full blast.

As soon as I get into the shower, and the water starts massaging me, I let out a relieved breath. Today was one big ball of stress that I wasn't ready for, and it sucked.

I'm glad that I was finally able to be honest about my past with the people I care about, and it's a weight off my shoulders. It does bother me that Ricky and his friends are still so hell bent on messing with me, but I can't let that ruin my life. .

"Turn that frown upside down, baby."

Turning my head, I find a naked Exton opening the shower door. I smile as I open my arms to him, burying my face against his chest as he pulls me in tightly.

"Thank you for coming after me," I murmur.

"Thank you for telling me the whole story," he responds. "Just know that if you run, I'm always going to follow. We're permanent, Arden. Not temporary."

I laugh softly against his chest. In retrospect, it's really hilarious that I ever thought that we were temporary. In my heart of hearts, I think we're forever. I'm just afraid to accept that because I don't want to be hurt again. What Ricky and his crew did was awful, but the pain of losing Exton would be devastating. I didn't know what true and all-encompassing love was until he came into my life—and now that I have it, I never want to let it go.

"What're you thinking?" he asks.

Considering my response, I reflect on all of the progress that I've made since he came into my life. Taking a deep breath, I decide not to run anymore. No more hiding—this is my life, and I'm taking charge.

Taking a step back, I look up into his eyes.

"I'm thinking about how much I love you," I answer honestly.

The look that flashes across his face is one of disbelief. Just when I start to panic, it's replaced by one of absolute joy.

"Never in a million years did I think that you'd admit that without me forcing the issue," he says. "I've been dying to tell you how much I love you, but I didn't want to scare you away. You're a tough nut, beautiful, but I wouldn't have it any other way."

My heart fills up with even more love for him. Snuggling back into his chest, I smile.

"Thank you for not giving up and letting me to run away."

"I'll never stop fighting for you, Beautiful. Not ever." he vows.

Just knowing that to him I'm worth all of the extra effort lets me know in a way that words never could that this man is the one. Even when I fell for Ricky's shit, I still never felt entirely secure. I never felt good enough or pretty enough for him.

With Exton, I feel beautiful. Even on days when I have issues with my appearance, deep down, I know that in his mind, I'm stunning. I've never been loved, ever, in a way that has made me feel so treasured. My mother, God bless her, loved and provided for me—but I wasn't what she wanted. My grandparents loved me, but I wasn't what they wanted for their child. I have always internalized the fact that the town bullying was my fault just for being born.

For the first time in my life, I'm the first choice. It's overwhelming, liberating, amazing and humbling, all at the same time. Exton makes me feel all of the best ING words, and I feel like the luckiest girl in the world.

"You ready to get clean before I make you dirty," he asks with a sexy chuckle.

Leaning back so that I can look up at him, I nod my agreement. "So ready," I laugh.

He takes control right away—as he always does. It's just another thing that I love about him. I'm safe and treasured—and now I know for sure, loved.

chapter nine

Arden

THE NEXT MORNING I wake up to the sound of Exton talking in the other room. I listen long enough to ascertain that he's on the phone with his attorney. After using the bathroom, brushing my teeth and slipping into his shirt, I head out into the living room to see what's up.

I find him pacing the room, and I can tell just by the way he's carrying himself that he's annoyed. Dressed in only his jeans—I'm wearing the shirt he had on yesterday—he looks sexier than ever. I get weak in the knees as I stare at him, and a sigh escapes me.

Looking over his shoulder, he smiles when he sees me.

"Listen, I've got to go. You've got my permission to hire the PI of your choice. I want to know who that really is in the photos and I want to sue the shit out of Ricky Greenway. If the girl in the photos is involved, we're suing her too. Fuck, I'll sue the whole town. Get me some answers."

After tossing the cell phone onto the coffee table, he strides across the room and pulls me into his arms.

"Good morning, beautiful."

Not giving me a chance to respond, he slides his fingers into my hair and tilts my head back before covering my lips with his. Wrapping my arms around his shoulders, I hold on as he kisses me senseless.

I moan and rub against him as he starts gliding his hands from my head down to my bottom. Grabbing onto me possessively, he lifts me off my feet. Taking the hint, I wrap my legs around his waist.

The feel of the mattress behind me startles me. Pulling my lips away from his, I let out a laugh. When I say he kisses me mindless, I mean it. I had no idea he was even walking us toward the bedroom.

"Do I amuse you, Miss Winger?"

Nodding my head in the affirmative, I smile. "I was so wrapped up in the kiss that I didn't even know you were bringing us down the hall."

Gripping the edge of his shirt, he quickly pulls it up and then over my head. "Good to know that I'm doing it right," he chuckles.

Reaching my hand out, I slide my fingers over his denim-covered cock. His strangled moan is music to my ears.

"You're definitely doing it right," I say huskily as I sink to my knees in front of him.

I could be asking a million and one questions right now about the situation with the fake pictures—but being with him is more important. Just knowing that it isn't me in the photos—even if no one else ever believes that—is a weight off my shoulders.

He takes half a step back to give me room to work, and I smile up at him. After undoing the snap and the zipper of his jeans, I pull them down his legs and help him step out of them. When they're off, I raise an eyebrow and smirk at him.

"Mm," I murmur. "Commando."

Gripping his shaft, I lean in and swirl my tongue around the tip of his cock, letting out a moan as the taste of him infiltrates my senses. Threading his fingers into my hair, he holds on as I start working him in and out of my mouth. Too big for me to ever dream of getting him past the back of my throat, I've perfected the art of working my fist on the bottom half of his shaft as I suck him so that he's being touched everywhere.

"Fuck, baby," he moans brokenly as I use my free hand to gently rub his balls. My own level of arousal escalates as I take in the sounds of his pleasure while I suck his beautiful cock. If there's a more powerful aphrodisiac than knowing that you're making your partner crazy with lust, I don't know what it is.

Letting go of the bottom of his shaft and releasing his balls from my grasp, I glide my hands up his thighs and reach around to grab his ass. He loves when I go 'hands free,' and the guttural sounding growl he lets out when I look into his eyes makes me feel like a million dollars.

"Arden," he whispers brokenly. "You always look so fucking sexy with my dick in your mouth."

My reply is a series of moans around his cock.

"Oh fuck, beautiful, you've got to stop," he growls at the same time he reaches behind him and takes my hands off his ass. As soon as he steps back, I lose him in my mouth.

"I wasn't finished," I pout.

Helping me to my feet, he tosses me onto the bed before crawling on top of me. "You might not have been finished, but I almost was."

Sliding his fingers across my drenched sex, he smiles when I let out a breathy gasp. "I'll be coming buried in this tight, perfect pussy," he says. "But you know that if you'd like to lick me clean after, that can be arranged."

My response is an eager nod, having recently discovered that I enjoy that almost as much as he does. I never could have imagined the kind of sex that Exton and I have. I trust him, which makes me willing to try pretty much everything. I know that he won't hurt me or take advantage, so I feel empowered to explore.

"So goddamn hot," he rasps as he slides two fingers inside of me and begins to rub circles on my clit with his thumb. "I love the way that sexy little tongue feels as it just barely brushes against me after I've come so fucking hard I can barely breathe. Love knowing that you're tasting us."

"Please," I whimper.

Pulling his fingers out of me, he trails both of his hands up my torso. Cupping one of my breasts in each hand, he rolls my nipples with his thumbs, watching my reaction intently. I love the way he watches and always seems to know just what I need.

"You're hot this morning," he observes.

"Yesss," I whisper.

"Can't wait, can you?"

My core clenches as he pinches both of my nipples. Shaking my head I answer simply. "Please. Now."

Nodding his head, he grins at me. "Turn over and lay flat. Keep your legs together."

I roll over quickly and do as he instructs.

"Lift up a bit to let me in," he growls from behind me.

Fisting the comforter below me I lift up. As he slides in, I forget to breathe. Setting his hand on my ass, he gently pushes me down.

"Don't move," he says. "I'll do all the work."

The position is new to me, but it takes me less than a minute to figure out that I'm not going to last long this way.

"You're so fucking tight," he moans as I clench against him.

The pressure on my mound with each thrust has me seeing stars, and I'm helpless to contain my cries of pleasure. When I feel his chest against my back as he raises my hair up off of my neck, I break out in gooseflesh.

Trailing his tongue along the back of my neck, he nibbles and kisses different spots as I breathlessly chant his name. When I feel a warm, wet finger tickling at my rear entrance, I stop breathing entirely.

"It's okay," he whispers against my ear. "I'll be gentle. Trust me, beautiful. This is going to make you come like crazy."

Taking a deep breath, I nod my head. His finger circles against my entrance at least a dozen times, and I shudder as my arousal spikes even higher.

"That's it, baby. Now I'm going to slide my finger in. Just relax and let it happen."

It's not the most comfortable thing as his finger passes the first ring. Only the fact that he's still thrusting slowly in and out of my core with his cock keeps me from tensing up entirely. Right when I feel his knuckle slip in, the discomfort shifts a bit. When he's finally all the way in and he starts moving his finger in and out, I finally understand why he said I would like it.

"Oh! Exton!"

"That's right, baby. You feel so fucking good, Arden. You're going to scream for me when you come all over my cock like a good girl, aren't you?"

"Yes!"

His thrusts take on a more desperate note as my cries get louder, and I barely contain screams as he works my pussy with his cock and my ass with his finger.

Full. I'm so fucking full. Add in the way that this position is making my clit throb and I'm a goner. I feel myself going over as I light up from the inside.

"I'm coming, I'm coming!" I scream.

My orgasm is just coming to an end when he pulls his finger out of me and grips my hips in his hands. Using them for leverage, he starts thrusting in and out as fast as he can.

The pressure of his cock going in and out as fast as it is has me on the verge of coming again, and it's almost too much.

"Please," I beg brokenly. "I can't."

"You can, beautiful. Squeeze that tight cunt and don't stop until you come," he growls.

As soon as I start to squeeze, I know I'm done for. In a matter of seconds, I'm coming again, hard.

"Fuck! Arden!"

When I feel the heat of his come inside of me as he releases, my core spasms in a second wave of orgasm. My body erupts in gooseflesh and I shiver uncontrollably as tears pour down my face and I let everything go.

"Fuck, baby. Why are you crying?"

Opening my eyes, I find that I'm now on my back and wrapped in Exton's arms. Shaking my head, I sniffle as I wipe at my eyes.

"They're g-g-good tears," I cry.

"I don't like it when you cry," he responds. "Whether they're good or not, I hate to see tears on that beautiful face. You're killing me, baby."

"I'm okay," I sniffle. "I just love you so much."

"I love you more," he says as he hugs me closer.

"I wanted to use my tongue on you," I half-laugh, half cry.

"Later, beautiful. We've got all the time in the world."

I'm the luckiest girl ever. As long as I have him, I can deal with anything.

chapter ten

Exton

THREE DAYS AFTER I got a statement out to the press about the fact that the photos circulating of my woman are fakes, Arden was adamant about going back to work.

"I can't hide," she'd argued. "I can't, and I'm not going to try. The pictures aren't of me and I have nothing to be ashamed of. Whether the press believes that or not is irrelevant. You and I know it isn't true. Our friends know. That has to be enough. I can't spend my life running anymore. This is my life and I'm happy. I'm done with letting Small Towne dictate my actions."

I wish that I had her outlook. She has the ability to compartmentalize things and move on, but I'm not there yet. It fucking kills me that she's had to learn how to walk away and keep on going after a lifetime of this kind of torture. No one deserves to be treated like garbage. Ever.

I've never been okay with bullying. It pisses me off whenever I see it happening—and working in Hollywood, I see it often. People treating their assistants like dog shit, actresses starting horrible rumors about their peers—you can see it all in LA, and it never gets any easier.

As pissed off as it normally makes me, this is worse. My attorney has an investigator looking for Ricky Greenway, but so far, they've pulled up exactly jack shit. He rolled out of Small Towne the day the photos were sold and as far as we can tell, he hasn't been back since.

Arden might be trying to move on, but every time there's a story online that says that we "claim" that the photos aren't of her, I struggle to control myself. When I see paparazzi following her and asking ridiculous questions, I want to punch someone or something. I've never felt this angry about anything—and that includes when my sex tape was everywhere and people were making jokes at my expense all the damn time. It's not fucking okay with me that Arden is being put through this, and I feel like I could snap at any moment.

Over the last two weeks she's shared so much about her upbringing and all the things that happened to her in Small Towne. I love that she's finally able to tell me everything, but every day my rage grows exponentially. I want—no, I need—to hurt the person that did the most damage to her.

The second that Greenway prick comes up from whatever hole he's escaped into, he'll be dealing with me directly.

I'm half asleep when I hear my cell phone vibrating on the nightstand. Normally, I'd let it go—but until I find out where that Greenway motherfucker is, I'm not missing a call. Disentangling myself from a sated and exhausted Arden, I snatch up my phone. When I see that it's my attorney, my pulse speeds up. It's after eleven—the fact that he's calling this late had better be a good sign.

Sliding my finger across the screen, I don't waste time with a greeting. "Tell me you've got something."

"I've got something."

Propping the cell between my shoulder and ear, I climb out of bed. After grabbing my discarded boxers, I leave the bedroom quietly so that I don't wake my woman up.

The second the door closes behind me I snap, "Where is he, Ray?"

"He's back in Small Towne and staying on a friends farm. Now that we know where he is, I can have him served—"

"No," I snap. "You won't be serving anything until after I talk to him. Email me everything you've got. I'll make arrangements and fly out tomorrow."

"As your attorney I have to advise you—"

"And as my friend, you know better than to try. What if that shit had happened to Darlene, Ray? Would you sit by and do nothing?"

He's silent for long enough that I know he's really giving my words consideration.

"No," he admits. "I wouldn't."

"Exactly. Email me that shit and I'll take care of it. You can feel free to serve him with a dozen lawsuits the second I'm on my way back to LA."

The second I've hung up with Ray, I pull Laz's number up and call him. When he answers, I get right to business.

"You're going to need the sous chef in charge tomorrow. We're taking a trip to Small Towne so that I can pay Ricky Greenway a visit."

Laz always has my back, no question about it, and I know this won't be an exception.

"Consider it done. What time do we roll out?"

"Give me a few hours to work out the details. The earlier we get out, the better—I'm not taking any chances that Pussy Greenway will do another runner."

I don't tell Arden that I'm going to Small Towne. I refuse to lie to her, ever, but I knew if I were to tell her that I'm doing this, she would try to talk me out of it. In the end, I simply tell her that I am going out with Laz and leave it at that. He and I are on the private jet I chartered just before nine this morning.

After landing in Bronson, not too far from where Arden went to college, we quickly get in the SUV I rented and make the rest of the journey to Small Towne. Pulling up to the house that the GPS leads us to, I turn off the ignition and turn to face Laz.

"You can come with, but if shit starts going down and he fights back, don't even think about jumping in until I'm finished with him."

"I got it, I got it," he answers tiredly. "You're going to knock this prick out and then we're going to head back to civilization."

My blood is boiling as I stomp up the porch to the front door of the farmhouse. Right now, my temper is controlling me. I know that's not ideal, but I can't calm myself down.

The door swings open and I immediately recognize the piece of shit that humiliated my woman. The picture the PI provided was from yesterday, and this loser hasn't changed his clothes. I see in his eyes the very instant that he recognizes me, and I can't contain the evil smile that I give him.

Yanking open the screen door, I step right up into his face. "Hello, Ricky. Seems you and I have something to talk about."

Raising his hands defensively in front of him, he shakes his head. "No man, I swear to God, I didn't do it! I had no idea where Ardy went—"

It's the fact that he dares to call her Ardy that snaps my temper like a brittle twig. My fist is slamming into the side of his face before I've really made the decision to do it.

"You don't fucking call her Ardy," I yell as I continue to throw punches.

The dumb fuck barely throws a punch back, instead going on the defensive and trying to block. I hear yelling and high-pitched screaming—a child, I think—going on in the background as I pummel him, but even that doesn't stop me.

"Stop," he yells. "Please, just stop! I didn't do it!"

I don't let up for one simple reason: because I can't. The rage that I feel toward this asshole is massive, and I want to fucking destroy him.

"Liar!"

I let loose a string of expletives as I'm pulled off of him, and I get as many jabs in as I can as we're separated.

Stumbling back, I'm shocked to find that the men that have pulled me off Ricky are in uniform. I don't even get to say a word before I'm in handcuffs. Laz is trying to talk the cops into letting me out, but they aren't having it. After telling him to shut his mouth before he's in cuffs too, they read me my rights.

chapter eleven

Arden

OPENING THE DOOR, I find Dante and Sabrina on the other side. Swinging it wide, I smile broadly as I gesture for them to come in.

"Exton's been out with Laz all day—"

"We need to sit down and talk."

I'm shocked by the serious expression on Dante's face, but instead of questioning him, I follow as he leads me into Exton's living room. Dropping down onto a chair, I wait for him to fill me in. As Sabrina takes a seat on the arm of the chair and sets a reassuring hand on my shoulder, my stomach sinks. Something is wrong.

Raking a hand through his hair, Dante lets out a frustrated sigh. "There's no easy way to say this, so I'm just going to give it to you straight. Exton's been arrested for assault. He's in jail."

Jumping from my seat I cry out in shock. "Why the hell are we sitting here? We need to go get him out!"

"There's nothing that we can do until tomorrow," he answers. "His bail hearing will happen in the morning. I need you to pack so that we can be there. I've got my pilot heading to the airport now."

Strictly Temporary

Looking over at Sabrina, I try to comprehend what's going on. "I don't understand—what? Why would we need to fly?"

"Because he's being held at the Small Towne police department."

∽⌒∽

I was a mess of nerves the entire way here. The number one spot—in fact, the only spot—on my list of places I never ever want to see again is Small Towne. Being back isn't ideal and, in all honesty, I'd be sick about it if I weren't so worried about Exton.

Fortunately, there are no hotels in Small Towne, so last night we stayed in Bronson. I didn't sleep a wink because I couldn't turn my head off. I hate that Exton is in jail, and I was beside myself all night because I couldn't see or speak to him.

Laz came to the hotel and talked to me for a long time, assuring me that Exton will be fine. His description of Exton beating the absolute shit out of Ricky didn't upset me in the least. Honestly, it wouldn't have been a negative at all if Exton didn't wind up behind bars.

Driving through Small Towne on the way to the Courthouse—a historical building right at the center of town—was almost more than I could take. When we got about a block away I saw the photographers lined up outside and I just about threw up.

Dante and Laz had both warned me that the entertainment press had started to show up, but being told and seeing it were two different things.

We got past the photographers and into the courthouse fairly quickly, all things considered. I am proud of myself for ignoring their rude questions and ridiculous speculations about what happened. Exton has taught me that it's best to say nothing and let his publicist handle it—so I'm following that.

As soon as we get inside, I hear the whispers and see people staring at me. I recognize several of the faces, and not one belongs to anyone I've missed. Looping her arm through mine supportively, Sabrina stays right by my side as we walk into the one and only courtroom.

The second we enter the room, I see Exton standing at the front with his attorney, a police officer, the judge, a man that I don't recognize—and Ricky Greenway. Stopping dead in my tracks, I swallow past the desert in my mouth. The sight of the bruising on his face and the black eye he's got is about the only thing welcome in having to see him again.

When he turns and sees me, he loses all the color in his face. Looking away from him in disgust, I'm just in time to see Exton look over his shoulder, presumably to see why Ricky suddenly looks like chalk. Raising his finger in a 'one minute' gesture, he turns back and says something to the group. After shaking the judge's hand and slapping his own attorney on the back, he comes straight to me.

He opens his arms and I run right into them, burying my face in his neck as he lifts me up in a tight hug.

"I'm sorry, beautiful. I didn't mean to worry you—"

Pulling back, I cover his mouth with my hand to halt his words.

"Don't you dare apologize for anything. All I care about is you. What happens now?"

Letting me go, he turns me around so that we're facing our friends and then wraps his arm around my shoulders.

"No charges," he says simply. "The Greenway prick doesn't want any of this. Turns out it wasn't him that pulled this photo bullshit, either."

Opening my mouth to ask who did it, I snap it closed when I hear Ricky say my name. My actual name, not Ardy like he always has before. Stepping out from Exton's arm, I spin on my heel and come face to face with Ricky.

I don't have the ability to be cordial where he's concerned. "What the hell do you want, Ricky?"

The years haven't been kind to him. He's the same age as I am, but he looks tired. He's got that hard living kind of look about him. I'm sure that the girls in town still love him—they always did—but right now I'm stunned that I ever thought he was attractive.

He seems surprised by the fact that I'm staring him down. Looking uncomfortable, he looks down at the floor before looking back up at me.

"I told your—erm, boyfriend—that I wanted to apologize, so here I am. I don't expect your forgiveness, but you deserve to know that I understand that what I did was wrong."

Shaking my head, I give him a dirty look. "You've never been sorry a day in your life," I say venomously. "You're a loser, Ricky Greenway, and you'll always be a loser. Take your apology and shove it up your ass."

His eyes are wide as I speak, and he looks mortified.

"I know I deserve that, Arden. I was a bad kid and a worse man. My son has Down's Syndrome," he explains. "Some of the town kids started making fun of him and that woke me up. All I care about is being a good father to my kids—and apologizing for what I did wrong is something I had to do."

I look to Exton for confirmation, and he nods once. Turning back to Ricky I snap, "If you really didn't sell those pictures, then who did it?"

Raking a hand through his hair, he shakes his head sadly. "It was Rhonda. It's *always* Rhonda. She left town after our son was diagnosed with Down's, and I don't see her but once a year now. I knew she was up to no good when she showed up at my house and tried to talk me into going to some tabloids and telling them some big lies about you. Didn't so much as look at our kids while she was there, either. Typical Rhonda—only cares about herself. I told her no, and she left off in a huff."

"I got a message from her sister two days later telling me that Rhonda sold some fake pictures and was telling people that they came from me. Second I saw the pictures, I recognized that they were of Rhonda. I knew shit was about to blow up, so I packed up my daughter and my son and took them down to Hank's parents' trailer at the beach, figured I'd put word out that anything she said came from me was bullshit. That plan didn't work cause I didn't know who the hell to call. Heard on the news that your boyfriend was going to sue me and I panicked because I can't be away from my kids. I'm all they've got."

"I didn't know how to get ahold of either of you and the press has been pokin' around. I had to come home because my boy needs to be in school. Decided to stay at Ivan's until everything blew over—and then your man showed up and beat my ass."

I can't believe what I'm hearing. I don't forgive Ricky—that's never going to happen—but I do feel horrible for his children. Rhonda has always been a selfish asshole and a complete nightmare. I can't imagine how sad having her for a mother would be.

"Where is Rhonda now?" I ask.

"Gave your man all the info that I've got. Best bet is to get in touch with her sister Ruby. Ruby's good people and she don't put up with Rhonda's shit. She's spent years tryin' to cut ties with Rhonda, but seein' as how she's in charge of their parents' money, she's never been able to get Rhonda to go away. With Ruby bein' the one holdin' the purse strings—eventually Rhonda always goes back to hold her up for more."

Crossing my arms over my chest, I stare him down. "I hope that you're being one hundred percent straight with us, Ricky. I accept your apology, but I'll never forgive or forget what you did. If you're pulling something here, I won't hesitate to beat your ass myself. I'm leaving Small Towne today, and it better be for the last time. If I have to come back and deal with you for any reason, it won't be pleasant. Understood?"

He nods so fast that he looks like a bobblehead. It's hard to process that the man I see before me is anything like the little punk I knew growing up. As much as I dislike him, I feel for his situation.

"Thank you, Arden. I really appreciate your takin' the time to hear me out. I hope you're happy in California, and I wish you nothin' but the best. You deserve it."

Spinning on is heel, he walks away without another word, and I'm glad to see the back end of him. For me, it's over. I'm not giving this town or the people who made my life so miserable another thought.

Turning back to Exton, I smile. "Let's get out of here and leave my past behind me, forever. From now on, I'm all about our future."

chapter twelve

Exton

IT'S BEEN ALMOST TWO months since we got back from Small Towne. Being there—even just for the short time that I was—gave me a better understanding of what Arden dealt with growing up. I hate everything that she had to deal with, but I'm thankful that she left it all behind and came to California.

Every day that I'm with her, I love her more. No hesitation and no reservations—this woman is my life. She's more than a spark, she's a generator and she started my heart.

We're on our way home—she officially lives with me now—from a two-week vacation on a private island. We loved spending all that time together, most of it naked. It's kind of hysterical that we spent all that time naked and my woman's skin is still porcelain pale. She wasn't kidding when she told me that she doesn't get any color.

I've been keeping a secret from her for the last month, and I'm anxious to get home to show her what I've done. As she snuggles against me in the back of the limo that's driving us home, she trails a finger up the inside of my thigh.

Growling low in my throat, I capture her sexy mouth in a kiss.

When we're both breathless, I pull away and trace her lower lip with my thumb. "None of that, beautiful. If we don't stop, I'll have you up against the door the second we walk into the house."

Her eyes dilate as she sucks in a breath before capturing my thumb with her teeth and nipping at it gently.

"What would be the problem with that?" she questions with a laugh. "Did I wear you out on vacation?"

"Not a chance," I chuckle. "I've got a surprise for you but I promise, the second I can, I'll be back inside of you."

"Ooh," she exclaims. "What surprise?"

Gesturing out the window I answer, "We're here, so you're about to find out."

After depositing our luggage in the foyer, I grab the black silk blindfold that I asked Sabrina to get me from the entry table. Dangling it from my finger, I hold it up to Arden.

"Put this on, baby."

Raising an eyebrow she giggles nervously. "Why?"

Dropping a quick kiss on her lips, I chuckle. "You'll see."

After she puts the blindfold on, I set my hands on her shoulders and walk her down the hallway. Walking her into the large room next to my office, I smile when I see it in person for the first time. The designer that Sabrina hooked me up with nailed it.

Bringing Arden to the center of the room, I lean in and whisper against her ear, "Are you ready?"

"Ready."

"Alright, baby. Here we go."

Walking around so that I can see her face, I pull the blindfold off gently. Her eyes fly around the room in wonder as her jaw drops. Turning in a slow circle, she takes it all in.

"Oh wow," she gasps as she takes in the floor to ceiling bookshelves that line the entire back wall. Dante's sister Dominique had a field day filling the shelves to the brim with romance novels. The beautiful reading nook in front of it is somewhere that I can see Arden spending a lot of time.

Looking at the desk that sits on the other side of the room across from the shelves, she walks over to it and traces her finger over the surface. Looking at the enormous iMac that's on the desk, she turns to me with a confused look on her face.

"I don't get it," she says. "You already have an office."

"I do," I say with a nod. "But you didn't. This is your office, beautiful. You can come in here and read or write whenever you want. I know you want to keep on working and I support that totally, but I also want you to explore your dream."

Tears are now running down her cheeks unchecked. Falling into my arms, she kisses me over and over again. "I love you, I love you, I love you," she whispers between kisses.

"I love you more. Look around and get to know your new office."

She goes from spot to spot, exploring every inch of the space. Running her hands along the bookshelves, she looks at the spines of her books. I bought her an iPad for our trip and she spent a lot of time reading. Seeing her enjoy something so thoroughly really made the vacation for me. The woman that I met who ran from everything is really living now, and I love her more than life itself.

Feeling my phone vibrate in my pocket, I smile as I pull it out and read the text. The final part of my surprise is in place.

"It's time to go for you to see your next surprise."

Eyes wide, she looks up at me in confusion. "There's more?"

"Yeah, baby. There's more. The best is always yet to come."

Linking her fingers with mine, I walk her down the hall to the front door. Opening it wide, I drink in the sound of her gasp when she sees the horse drawn Cinderella style carriage that's sitting in my driveway.

Covering her mouth with her hand, she stares in shock as my nephew Jack helps Vivi climb out of the carriage. She's absolutely adorable; all dressed up in a Princess Belle costume. Skipping over to Arden and I, she giggles when she sees how surprised Arden looks.

Launching herself up into my arms, she smiles over at Arden. "See that fairytale carriage?" she asks her.

Nodding her head Arden answers, "I do. What's it doing here?"

"It's here to take you for a ride," Vivi answers. "But you have to believe in fairytales to get in. Do you believe?"

My heart starts pounding harder as two tears roll down Arden's cheeks before she quickly wipes them away. Smiling at Vivi, she nods.

"I forgot how for a long time. But thanks to your Uncle E, I got it back. I believe."

"Yay!" Vivi exclaims. "That means you can get in now."

After kissing my cheek and then leaning out to kiss Arden, Vivi asks to be put down. The second her feet are on the ground, she skips to where Dante, Sabrina and Laz are now standing, right next to the carriage.

Taking Arden's hand, I lead her to the carriage. Stopping just outside of the door, I grab the blue velvet box that Cooper is holding out to me. Turning to face my beautiful girl, I drop to one knee before her. Opening the box, I show her the enormous—but still tasteful, I've been assured—princess cut diamond.

"Arden, the second I saw you, I knew you were different. I fall in love with you more every day and I want to spend my life with you. Will you marry me?"

I breathe a sigh of relief the second I see that she's nodding her head. "Yes," she cries happily. "Yes!"

After sliding the ring onto her finger, I stand up and kiss her as everyone applauds. Keeping it PG-*ish* on account of the fact that my niece and nephews are watching, I pull back with a laugh. "Want to go for a ride?"

Wiping away tears, she smiles. "I really, really do."

Taking her hand, I help her up and into the carriage. After settling into my seat, I pull her into my arms as we start moving. Los Angeles looks nothing like the Enchanted Forrest, but I have to admit that it looks pretty damn good from the inside of a carriage.

chapter thirteen

Arden

A CONTENTED SIGH ESCAPES me as I take off my wedding shoes. The second I tried them on, Sabrina declared that they were perfect. They definitely were, but now my feet are in agony. I've really got to stop letting her talk me into sky high, fuck me heels. She can handle the pain, but I can't—especially not when I'm swollen.

At Exton's insistence, we went all out for the wedding. The guest list was small, but it was a real wedding from beginning to end. I had mentioned the elopement word once, right after we got engaged, and he'd quickly shut that down. In no uncertain terms he told me that our marriage was going to be real and forever, and that he wanted our children to be able to see our wedding pictures. It took six months to plan everything down to the last detail, but seeing how it all came together today was amazing.

I wound up in a gown that makes me feel like a princess, something that made Vivi giggle when I said it earlier today. Of course, as my flower girl, she was wearing a smaller version of my dress. Right before it was time for the wedding to start, she told me that she thought maybe she wants to be the very first princess cowgirl. Now that I believe in fairytales again, I think that anything is possible.

Rubbing my shoulders, Exton leans in and kisses the back of my neck. "Feet are killing you?" he asks with a laugh.

"God yes," I answer honestly.

"Once I get you out of this dress, I'll make you forget all about that," he promises.

Anyone that tells you that getting in or out of a wedding dress is quick is lying. It takes quite a few minutes to get the dress off. When we finally get it off, I smile when I hear Exton's harsh inhalation as he takes in what I'm wearing. The sexy bustier, lace thong, and thigh high stockings make me feel amazing, and the look on his face tells me that I nailed it.

"You're about to get fucked hard, Mrs. Alexander," he says wickedly.

Walking toward the bed, I turn and smile at him over my shoulder. "Promises, promises."

Coming up from behind, he wraps his arm around my waist and pulls me against his rock solid chest.

"Trust me," he rasps. "That's a promise I'm going to fulfill."

Turning me around so that I'm facing him again, he trails his fingers up and down my arms.

"I missed you last night, beautiful. While I was tossing and turning, trying to get to sleep without you in my arms, I had lots of time to fantasize about what I'd do to you tonight."

Tilting my head to the side, he begins kissing my exposed neck. When I whimper and try to grind myself against him, he just chuckles. Turning my head the other way, he kisses the other side. Nibbling against a particularly sensitive spot, he sucks in. The pressure the suction goes directly to my core, and I clench my inner muscles as I feel myself get wetter.

Turning me around, he immediately pulls me into a kiss. Our tongues slide hotly together as our hands roam each other's bodies. Grabbing the lapels of his tuxedo, I help him take it off. Wanting—no, needing—more, I tear at the buttons of his shirt. Covering my hands, he pulls back.

"Feeling desperate, beautiful?"

Tracing my fingers over my kiss-swollen lips, I nod. "I always feel so desperate for you," I murmur.

Letting out a groan, he works quickly to get his cufflinks off. A gift from me for today, they're platinum and are engraved with our intertwined initials. After getting them off, he walks over to the dresser and sets them down carefully in the middle. Making quick work of it, he divests himself of his clothing.

More desperate for him than ever, I lick my lips when I see his beautiful cock. I'm horny all the time now and not seeing him last night almost killed me. When he gets in front of me, he runs his hands over the front of my bustier.

"This is sexy as all hell," he rasps, "But I want suck on your perfect fucking nipples while you ride my dick."

After helping me out of the bustier, he cups my breasts in his hands. Tracing each of his thumbs around a nipple, he smiles when I shiver. He kisses me again, quickly and deeply before he begins trailing wet kisses down my body.

Dropping to his knees on the floor, he traces his tongue up and down the insides of my thighs. I whimper when he runs his tongue over the lace of panties, and he responds with a sexy growl. Grabbing either side of my panties, he rolls them down my legs and then helps me step out of them.

"Sit down on the bed," he instructs.

I comply quickly, no hesitation. Spreading my legs, he positions them on his shoulders the way he likes. Hovering over my drenched center, he smiles up at me. "You smell so good, baby."

I cry out when he runs his tongue from my opening to my clit at least a half dozen times. "Mm," he groans. "So wet, and it's all for me."

Of their own volition, my hands fist in his hair as he begins working me over with his tongue. He knows my body almost better than I do now, and he knows just what to do to bring me to the edge and then pull back before I come.

I start shaking when he slides two fingers inside of my aching sex and starts making the come-hither motion with his fingers.

"God, please!" I yell out.

I feel him growl against me as he picks up speed with his tongue and his fingers. My head thrashes back and forth as I dissolve under him with a cry of pleasure. When he's wrung every possible moment out of my orgasm, he takes my legs off his shoulders and begins working his way back up my body.

I shiver and shake when he dips his tongue into my belly button, then cry out as he gently bites first one nipple and then the other. Grabbing his hair, I pull him away. "So sensitive," I moan. "Too much."

Nodding his understanding, he climbs over me and settles between my legs. After running the tip of his cock against my opening and getting himself wet, he begins to slide in. The first thrust is always amazing—that full feeling as my pussy struggles to take all of him in. When he finally settles against me as deep as he can go, we both let out sounds of pleasure.

Hovering over me, chest to chest and joined so intimately, he smiles down at me before rubbing his nose against mine. "It's official now," he murmurs. "You're my wife—my forever. I love you so fucking much Mrs. Alexander."

Wrapping my arms and legs around him, I hug him tightly. "I love you too, Mr. Alexander."

I hold on tight as he begins a series of hard and deep thrusts, each one designed to make me crazy. I cry out over and over again as he rubs against my clit with his finger. Covering my mouth with his, he kisses me senseless as he fucks me stupid.

Only when he's gotten three orgasms out of me, and I'm begging him to come, does he let go. I clench against him as he fills me with his hot seed, shivering in the aftermath of our loving. I snuggle into him for a few minutes as drowsiness takes over. As my eyes drift shut, I decide to give myself a few minutes of rest.

It feels like a few minutes have passed when I come to and feel him tracing lazy circle around my stomach. Covering his hand with mine, I squeeze gently. Now's the perfect time to give him my other wedding present. I just have to sit up and be a little more alert.

"You didn't eat much at the reception," he says huskily. "It's my job to make sure that my family gets what they need. Think baby Alexander could go for a midnight snack?"

Gasping, I sit straight up and find him sitting on the bed next to me with an enormous smile on his face.

Completely awake now, I gape at him in disbelief. "How did you know? I was planning to surprise you tonight!"

"Baby, please," he says with a laugh. "I know every inch of this body. I've been watching you like a hawk ever since you stopped taking birth control. The second the wonder twins started getting bigger, I knew we had a baby on the way."

I'm laughing as I playfully smack his arm. "You can't call my boobs the wonder twins now that we're having a baby," I giggle.

"Not gonna call them the wonder twins in front of our kids," he says with a chuckle. "But when it's you and me, I'm still calling them that. They're fucking amazing."

There really aren't words to explain how much I love this crazy man. He's everything I dreamt about—and more, to be honest—all those years ago when I started reading love stories and envisioned what I wanted.

Falling into his arms, I smile as he slides his lips over mine and kisses me breathless. It just doesn't get any better than this.

epilogue

"ALRIGHT, MCKENNA. YOU READY to see Mommy read her book to some very special readers?"

Clapping her chubby hands together, my daughter gives me a toothy smile. "Momma! Books!" she giggles happily.

Walking into the room, I take a seat on the floor next to Sabrina and Vivi. We all applaud as my wife steps out, and I blow a kiss to her as she walks slowly to her seat. At eight months pregnant with our son, she's not moving at high speed anymore, but she's never been more beautiful to me.

She started writing her book a few months into her pregnancy with McKenna. What started as a daydream quickly turned into something huge. To date, it's sold more than two million copies, and there's already a movie in production.

After being introduced by her publisher, Arden smiles and waves at the crowd of clapping children and their parents.

"I wrote this book for my daughter McKenna and my niece, Viviene. It's called No Ordinary Princess."

"Once upon a time . . ."

about the author

Ella Fox is the USA Today Bestselling Author of Consequences of Deception, The Hart Family series & many other sexy and exciting books.

Ella loves music, photography and comedy movies. She's an all around goofball. She grew up loving to read, especially romance. That's not surprising considering the fact that her mom is USA Today Bestselling Author Suzanne Halliday.

LIKE me on Facebook & you'll never miss a release or any of my fabulous giveaways!

Facebook.com/EllaFoxAuthor

Follow me on Twitter: @AuthorEllaFox

Visit my website and sign up for my mailing list:
www.authorellafox.com

strictly temporary playlist

Breakaway Kelly Clarkson
Stronger Kelly Clarkson
Fighter Christina Aguilera
Easier to Run Linkin Park
Not Myself Tonight Christina Aguilera
Secrets OneRepublic
Over My Head The Fray
She Will Be Loved Maroon 5
Please Don't Leave Me P!nk
Let Love In The Goo Goo Dolls
Halo Beyoncé
All of Me John Legend

    You can follow the Strictly Temporary playlist on Spotify

acknowledgements

Thank you to all of my BOOK BABES! Love you ladies!

Thank you to Lisa Schilling Hintz from The Rock Stars of Romance for being the most organized and on top of things person I know. Lisa does my blog tours & they are amazing. I'm blessed to have her in my life.

Thank you to Stacey Ryan Blake, the formatter from heaven. She takes my wonky looking documents and makes them look like masterpieces. I am so happy to have found her!

Thank you to my editor, Gemma Rowlands, for being with me all the way. She puts up with my crazy without even batting an eyelash.

Thank you to Sara Eirew for the amazing cover photos for the Strictly Temporary books. They were perfect!

Thank you to Sommer Stein for creating two phenomenal and absolutely gorgeous covers for these books. You rock!

Special and incredibly sincere thanks to Dena Marie from Fiction Fangirls, Nancy Miller, Tara & Dawn from Two Unruly Girls with a Romance Book Buzz, Yaya from After Dark Book Lovers, Lara Ross Petterson, Kathy Bankard, Christina Gobin from Books Unhinged, Wendy Colby, Sian Davies, Bethany Castanada, and Jennifer Inglehart.

To the author peers that rock my socks off. Each and every one of them makes me proud to be an Indie, and even prouder to have them as friends. Crystal Reynolds, Tessa Teevan, Kristi Webster, Rochelle Paige, Rachel Brookes, Elle Jefferson, Tijan Meyer, Jay McLean, KC Lynn, Tracey Frazier, Elle Christensen, Anne Mercier, Debra Anastasia, Monica Robinson, Beth Ehemann, Anne Jolin, Mary Elizabeth, Stylô Fantome, Kate Canterbary, SVC Ricketts, and my mom, Suzanne Halliday.

To EVERY blogger who takes the time to read and review books- THANK YOU. Bloggers work their asses off, FOR FREE. They spend their own money to do giveaways and run their blogs, and they don't get enough respect for the hard work that they put in. From the bottom of my heart, I thank you all.

I always miss people in the acknowledgements and it drives me nuts. If I slipped up, just know that I do appreciate you—and I'll get you on the next one.

Xo xo- Ella

Other books by Ella Fox

The Hart Family Series:
Broken Hart
Shattered Hart
Loving Hart
Unbroken Hart
Missing Hart
Finding Hart

The Renegade Saint Series:
Picture Perfect
Twist of Fate

The Catch Series:
Catch My Fall

The Deception Series:
Consequences of Deception